O9-AID-837

Weekly Reader
Children's Book Club
EDUCATION CENTER • COLUMBUS 16, OHIO

Presents

RIDE LIKE AN INDIAN!

by

HENRY V. LAROM

A 1958 Selection of the
WEEKLY READER
Children's Book Club
EDUCATION CENTER, COLUMBUS 16, OHIO

Also by Henry V. Larom

BRONCO CHARLIE

MOUNTAIN PONY

MOUNTAIN PONY AND THE ELKHORN MYSTERY

MOUNTAIN PONY AND THE PINTO COLT

MOUNTAIN PONY AND THE RODEO MYSTERY

RIDE *like an* INDIAN!

by Henry V. Larom

Illustrated by Wesley Dennis

WHITTLESEY HOUSE

McGraw-Hill Book Company, Inc.
New York Toronto London

To Tommie Ingersoll

The author wishes to express his grateful appreciation to Dale Wing, Sioux Indian, brother alumnus from Montana State University and now a relocation officer for the Bureau of Indian Affairs, for his expert help in all matters pertaining to Indians in this book.

First edition
Library of Congress Catalog Card Number: 58-6688
Manufactured in the United States of America
American Book–Stratford Press, Inc., New York

Published by Whittlesey House
A division of the McGraw-Hill Book Company, Inc.

WEEKLY READER
Children's Book Club
Edition, 1958

Contents

CHAPTER ONE

The Dreamy Race Horse

"Last one to reach Spring Creek is a tenderfoot," Garth said, pulling up his big bay horse.

Although most of them had been riding for weeks and were eager to run their horses, Jerry Phillips, trailing along the road behind them, had been on the dude ranch only a few days. His back hurt, his legs ached, his spine was sore, and he didn't want to race at all.

"Come on up with the rest of us," said Muriel, a slim blonde riding a sorrel. "Maybe old Applesauce will keep up this time."

Jerry hammered with his heels until his horse drew up alongside hers. He knew Applesauce would never keep up because he was known as "the kid pony," the pony for beginners—the old, safe horse that nobody else wanted to ride.

"Are you ready?" Garth asked, holding in his big bay.

"Sure!"

"On your mark. . . . Get set. . . ." Garth leaned forward in the saddle. "Go!"

Jerry kicked with his heels, and Applesauce jumped forward so fast that Jerry had to grab the saddle horn. Hoofs rattled on the roadway. Dust flew. The wind whistled past his ears. Jerry bounced in the saddle, then realized suddenly that he was leading, that Applesauce was ahead of everybody else. The mane lay flat against the horse's neck. His ears were back, his tail straight out behind. Jerry was so excited that he forgot his legs were sore. This was riding at last and he was ahead! Jerry hung on and laughed into the wind.

But a moment later, he felt a change in the horse's rhythm. Applesauce was slowing up. First Garth went by and yelled, "So long, slowpoke!" Then one by one the others passed him until even Muriel, the youngest of all except for himself, loped by on her sorrel pony.

Jerry pulled up on the reins, and Applesauce stopped running. It wasn't any use, Jerry thought. Applesauce was too slow, and it might hurt the old skate to gallop such a long way. Applesauce seemed glad to forget the whole thing. He dropped his head down, waggled his ears, blew a bit of dust out of his nose, and reached for some bunch grass by the roadside.

Jerry dragged the pony's head up again and tried to keep him from wandering around the road as they headed toward the ranch. He knew he looked funny, poking along on the sleepiest horse of all, the only one with big brown spots on its rump. And now that he had actually run in a race and even been ahead for a few hundred yards, he thought it was time for him to get out of the "kid-pony" class.

He wondered what it would be like to ride a real horse, an Indian pony, for instance. He had read a great deal about Indians, about the Sioux and the Cheyennes and the Nez Percés. It was Chief Joseph of the Nez Percés who had developed the horse with spots on its rump called an apaloosa. Jerry smiled. Perhaps old Applesauce was a Nez Percé way back. Brown in front, white in the middle, and white on the rump except for the big brown spots the size of silver dollars, Applesauce sure looked Indian, Jerry thought, even if he did waggle his ears like a mule and wander all over the road.

Jerry wished that he were an Indian in the old days —racing an apaloosa across the plains with the wind in his ears, riding into a buffalo herd, running races against the other braves. . . .

"Hey, Dreamy, pull up that race horse. It's time for lunch."

Jerry looked up and saw that while he had been thinking about Indians, Applesauce had arrived at the ranch. Garth and the others had already turned their horses into the big corral and were sitting on the fence laughing at him. When Applesauce, his neck sagging and his eyes half closed, finally lumbered to a stop in front of the saddle house, even Chuck Wallace, the corral boss, smiled a little.

"I was lost for a couple of hours," Jerry said, trying

to make a joke of it. "But my faithful mustang brought me home."

"Good old Dreamy," Garth said. "What do you care? You've probably got a book hidden under the saddle blanket."

Jerry dismounted and pulled off his saddle. The kids had begun to call him "Dreamy" because he carried books around and read a good deal. It made him angry.

"You going to ride that wild stallion in the races?" Garth asked.

"What races?"

The others laughed. "Gee, haven't you heard about them?" Muriel asked. "They've been posted on the saddle-house wall for two days."

Jerry saw the notice then. It said that there would be an O-Mock-See two weeks from the following Saturday. "O-Mock-See" was an Indian word meaning "games on horseback." There would be stake races, barrel races, and —most important of all—a grand quarter-mile race for young people. "This race is open to all guests under sixteen," he read. "Contestants must ride the regular horses assigned them by the corral boss. They may ride Eastern or Western fashion, using any saddle rig they choose. . . ." Jerry read on and his heart sank. What chance would he have riding Applesauce? He'd never make a showing against Garth or Ted Jackson and the others.

"Hey, Jerry!" He turned and saw that the others had gone, all but Muriel, who was beckoning him with a finger.

"Yeah?" Jerry didn't feel much like talking to her.

"Look, Jerry," Muriel said, "why don't you ask Chuck Wallace for another horse? Gee, you'll never get anywhere with that kid pony."

Jerry gazed at Applesauce, who, wanting to roll, was sniffing at the ground like an old beagle hound. "You've got something there," he said. "But do you think I ride well enough to ask for something better?"

"Sure," Muriel said.

Jerry noticed that the corral boss still leaned against a gatepost. He was a famous cowboy and rodeo rider. He knew his horses, and he watched over each one of them like a doting mother. If you abused your horse or brought him in hot, he could put you "afoot" for the day. He picked out your saddle and bridle. He decided which horse you rode. And because his word was law in the corral, all the young people were just a little bit afraid of him.

Jerry and Muriel walked over to him, and Jerry said, "Do you think maybe I can ride well enough to get a better horse pretty soon?"

Chuck didn't move. He didn't change his expression. He looked at Jerry and Muriel. Then he stared at Applesauce, who was rubbing his nose against a foreleg. "Nope," he said.

"Gee, why not?" Muriel asked. "Jerry rides real well now, Chuck. He even ran in a race and—"

"You been racin' your horses and gettin' 'em hot?" Chuck broke in.

Muriel blushed under her tan. "Well, not exactly. Just a little bit on the road and—"

"Runnin' 'em in all them rocks, huh?" Chuck asked.

"Well . . . yes . . . a little." Muriel was scared now. She was afraid they would all be put afoot for the rest of the day and it would be her fault.

"If you don't race 'em, Jerry's horse can keep up," Chuck said.

"But he doesn't," Jerry said. "He just doesn't!"

"Ride him awhile. Make him," Chuck said.

"But Chuck. . . ."

Muriel was going to try again, and Jerry didn't want a girl to fight for him. "That's all right, Muriel," he said. "But thanks for trying."

He took off his saddle, picked up his bridle reins and led Applesauce toward the corral to turn him loose. It was hot in the Wyoming sun. The snow on the mountain peaks glistened. Dust rose from the horse herd as a couple of mares kicked at each other, and Jerry, looking around him, wondered how long it would be before he could really enjoy it. All his life he had wanted to come West and ride horses. At last his family had given him this chance, and now it didn't seem like much fun—not with an old kid pony like Applesauce.

He was leaning against the corral gate and watching a little colt who was nudging at its mother for a drink of milk, when he felt something soft and warm at the back of his neck. It bunted him gently, pushing his Stetson over his eyes. Jerry turned and stared at Applesauce, who was pushing his nose into Jerry's shoulder. He was saying, plain as day, "Take my bridle off, boss. It itches, and I want to get in there and roll."

Jerry smiled. Applesauce was kind of a character at that, he thought. "But I do wish," he mumbled, "that you were a very fast Indian horse, too."

"He is," a voice said.

Jerry pulled Applesauce's head up and peered under it. Who was that?

"He's an Indian pony from the reservation." Jerry saw a boy of about his own age leaning against the fence. He had dark, sunburned skin, very black hair, and big black eyes. Jerry could see that he was not a guest at the ranch. He wore an old pair of torn blue jeans, a cotton shirt, and he was carrying two big pails of slops for the pigs to eat.

"How do you know he's Indian?" Jerry asked.

The boy put down the pails. "He's got the Box B reservation brand on his right shoulder. I know the horse. My dad sold him to the ranch."

"Do you know a lot about Indians?" Jerry, asked hopefully.

"I ought to," the boy said. "I *am* one."

"Gee!" Jerry was surprised. Somehow, he had always thought of Indians as wearing feathers and blankets the way they did in the movies. "And you say Applesauce is a real Indian pony?"

"You bet. Fast too. A race horse."

"What?" Jerry couldn't believe his ears.

"Sure," the Indian said, "a good quarter-miler. I'll bet he could beat these dude horses right now."

"You mean . . ." Jerry was so excited that he thought he might jump right out of his cow boots. "You mean that maybe I could make him win a race like the one we're going to have here in a couple of weeks?"

"You might." The Indian boy's eyes lit up like candles. "You just *might* . . . if you could ride like an Indian."

"But . . . but . . ." Jerry wondered if he was just dreaming as usual. "How could I ever learn to do that in three weeks?"

"Well," the Indian boy gave Jerry a shy grin. "Maybe I could help you . . . if you want me to. . . ."

CHAPTER TWO

Secret Training

"That would be wonderful," Jerry said. "Only. . . ." He thought of the other horses—of Garth's big bay, of Ted's chunky palomino, and of Muriel's fast little sorrel. It would be fine to beat them. Then he looked at old Applesauce, with his spotted rump, his waggling ears, and sad brown eyes. He was standing spraddle-legged against the fence, rubbing his forehead against a post, still trying to get the bridle off. "Isn't he pretty darn old to race?"

"Oh, he's about twelve, I guess," the Indian boy said. "But shucks! He'd still be fast in a kid's race."

Jerry wanted to believe him. Here was an Indian boy who had ridden all his life. He had probably owned horses of his own and been out on the range in early spring to see the little colts born in the sagebrush. But he was wrong about Applesauce. "If Applesauce is so fast," he asked, "how come Garth can pass me, and all the other boys, and even Muriel on that little sorrel?"

The Indian boy lowered his eyes and scraped the edge

of his old work shoe in the dust. "If I told you," he said, "you'd get mad."

"No I wouldn't," Jerry said hastily. "Honest I wouldn't."

"Well," the Indian boy looked up. "That old pony's been duded to death."

"Duded!" Jerry scratched his head. "Oh, you mean that he's so gentle and so many beginners start their riding on him that he goes to sleep, huh?"

The Indian boy nodded. "That's it. He's gentle. Why, shucks, he's had four-year-olds riding him this summer. They can't make him go."

"Neither can I," Jerry said ruefully, "except that when we started that race this morning, he got off fast. We were ahead for a little while."

"Sure," the Indian boy grinned. "I bet you've got the fastest-starting horse in the valley. But he won't go for a dude rider. He's learned how to loaf and he enjoys it. But if an Indian rode him, he'd go—and fast."

"Then you ride him in the race," Jerry said eagerly. "Show them how the Indians do it."

"Nope!" The Indian shook his head, but his deep eyes glittered. "I'd sure like that, but those races are for ranch guests only." He looked embarrassed again. "It was sure nice of you to offer me your horse, though."

Suddenly Jerry felt a warmth inside. He thought that the Indian liked him, and here was a chance to have a friend—an Indian friend.

"Well, anyway, maybe we could get a real Indian *horse* to win," he said.

As they went on talking, they became so interested that Jerry forgot to go to lunch. Instead, he helped the Indian boy feed slops to the pigs, pitch hay into the horse barns, and throw grain to the chickens. He discovered that the Indian's name was Sam, that he loved to read books about Indians, and that his father, a chief, had sent him to work on the ranch while the chief and his wife ran a string of race horses at the various fairs and rodeos in Montana and Wyoming.

"Say," Sam said, as they were passing the grain bin, "have you got any money?"

"I've got my allowance," Jerry said.

"Then you better buy some oats for Applesauce," Sam said. "Let's feed him now. It'll give him more pep, and you can pay for it at the end of the month."

They took Applesauce into the feed barn and gave him a can of oats. Jerry had never seen the old horse enjoy himself so much. He nudged the oats around with his nose, moistening them until he had a mess that looked almost like the oatmeal Jerry ate for breakfast, and when he had finished, he was so grateful that he laid his head on Jerry's shoulder and blew moist grains into Jerry's ear.

"Look," Sam said finally, "can you start training about four o'clock this afternoon?"

"Sure."

"All right. But remember that you won't be able to

ride with the other kids during the day. We'll have to do this all in secret or everybody will try to copy you."

"What do you mean?"

"Well, you're going to have to ride Indian fashion—no saddle, no chaps, no heavy boots. If your dude friends see you, they'll do the same thing. You'll lose an advantage. And we mustn't let Applesauce get tired either. We've got to build him up."

Jerry knew what the others would think when he refused to ride with them. They would call him "Dreamy." Garth, the leader, would laugh at him. But then, if he could learn to ride bareback. . . . He saw himself stripped to the waist, brown, hard, galloping across the plain on a fast apaloosa, yelling the war cry of the Sioux. . . .

"Sure, I'll keep it a secret," he said.

For some reason that Jerry didn't quite understand, Sam's black eyes became deadly serious. "Promise?" he asked, looking hard at Jerry.

"I promise," Jerry said. "Where'll I meet you?"

"In that cutover hayfield, the one that's over by the rimrock," Sam said. "Nobody's likely to see us there."

That afternoon Jerry stayed away from the corrals until he thought the others had left. Then he saddled up Applesauce and headed for the hayfield. Following the directions Sam had given him, he rode a narrow wood road through the cottonwoods. He moved slowly and stopped now and then to listen. It wouldn't do to be followed, he

thought. If Garth and the others ever realized what he was up to, they would be after him in no time.

When he reached the hayfield, he noticed that it was cut off on three sides from the rest of the ranch by trees, while the fourth was sagebrush country which rose in waves until it hit the towering rimrocks that formed the edge of the valley. A mighty good place for secret training, he thought.

Seeing no one, Jerry pulled up and listened. He heard the faint rustle of leaves as the wind stirred the trees. In the distance, a magpie squawked once. Then all was silence.

"Get off that horse!"

Jerry jumped half out of the saddle. Then he turned and saw Sam standing only 10 feet away.

"Gee, you scared me," he said.

"Some of us Indians can still move real quiet," Sam said, grinning. "Pull off your saddle, and I'll show you how to ride bareback."

Jerry slid the saddle off, and Sam took the reins and wrapped them around the pony's neck. "To mount," he said, "you have to jump high, then swing your leg over."

Sam was pretty small, Jerry thought, and Applesauce was a fairly tall horse. But Sam took a grip on the mane with his right hand and then jumped, light as a squirrel, across the horse's back.

Applesauce's ears sprang back for an instant as though he were surprised. Then his head came up and the ears cocked forward. He seemed to come alive all over, and his neck arched with excitement. "Now you kick him right into a lope," Sam said, and he dug the pony's ribs with his heels.

Applesauce jumped forward into a slow gallop and loped out into the field with his head high and his tail flying. Jerry almost laughed with excitement. No longer did Applesauce wander from side to side hunting for grass. He didn't look like an old skate. It seemed to Jerry that the horse had dropped five years from his life and had never

been a kid pony at all. And Sam sat the horse as easily as a cocklebur in a pony's mane. Riding free, balancing easily on the pony's back, he seemed part of the horse, and when he touched his heels to the apaloosa's flank, the horse shot ahead like an arrow.

Sam loped the pony around a haystack, then up and down the field several times, riding easily, never pushing the horse hard, but letting him canter gently. Then he pulled up in front of Jerry. "He's still pretty dead on his feet," he said, slipping off the horse's back. "But I think he'll come out of it in time for the race. Now you try."

"Dead, huh," Jerry said ruefully. "I hope I'm able to ride him when he comes *alive*." He put the reins around the pony's neck.

"Jump as high as you can," Sam said, "then get that right leg over."

Jerry crouched down, grabbing the horse's mane with his free hand, and jumped. He got his stomach across the horse's back, but his right leg didn't go high enough. It stuck in the middle of Applesauce's rump. Applesauce was surprised. He showed the whites of his eyes. This guy didn't ride like the last one. Something was wrong. Not knowing what to do, he broke into a trot.

Jerry struggled vainly to get the leg over. The trotting shook him, and the leg slipped back. As Applesauce ambled down the field, Jerry hung, like a great sack of flour, across the horse's back.

Sam ran after them. But he was laughing so hard that it took quite a while to catch up.

"Whoa," he said, at last, grabbing the reins, and Jerry finally slipped to the ground. "You'll have to do better than that. Applesauce thinks he's a pack horse bringing home the elk meat."

Jerry sat up and rubbed his stomach. "Well, I got part way on," he said, grinning. "Hold the reins this time, Sam, so Applesauce can't get away, and I'll try again."

This time, with Sam hanging on to Applesauce, Jerry made it, and found himself on top of the horse at last.

"How does it feel?" Sam asked.

"Like sitting on top of a loose barrel," Jerry said. It was mighty different from riding in a saddle. Jerry missed the horn in front to grab on to, and the cantle in back that held him in. But most of all he missed the stirrups. His legs hung loose and gave him no purchase. There was nothing to keep him from bouncing on the horse's spine. He felt that the slightest jolt would send him flying between the pony's ears.

"All right, kick him into a walk," Sam said, and Jerry touched his heels to Applesauce gingerly. Applesauce moved ahead. "Grip with your knees and hang on to his mane, but try to balance yourself as much as possible. Balance is just about the whole thing in bareback riding." Jerry hung on to the mane with both hands and clutched with his knees until his legs ached.

"Lift the reins!" Sam shouted. "No wonder the horse is half asleep. Lift the reins."

Jerry lifted the reins, but he hung on to the mane with his other hand, and with Sam trotting along behind, he walked the horse up and down the field. Gradually, it began to seem less strange to him. He could feel the rhythm of the horse's muscles moving under him. He began to loosen his knee grip and to balance himself a little on the horse's back.

"Now," Sam said, "the next thing to do is to lean forward a little and kick hard with your heels. Get Applesauce into a lope. Not a trot. A lope, Jerry."

"O.K.," Jerry said, uncertainly. "A lope it is." He took a hard grip on the mane, leaned forward, and kicked.

Applesauce didn't know what to make of the load he was carrying. His rider felt like a dude, so he broke into a slow jog trot. Each jog hit Jerry on the spine. He gripped with his knees. He hung on like grim death to the mane, but his spine hit so hard, he thought he must be sitting on a pile driver.

"Kick him!" Sam shouted, running after them. "Kick him into a lope, a gallop. Kick *hard*!"

Jerry thought he was going to split in two, but he kicked just as hard as he could.

Then, as Applesauce broke into a canter, the pounding stopped. It was like riding a rocking horse, Jerry thought. He still gripped with his knees, he still hung onto the mane, but just the same, as the horse loped down the field, Jerry began to realize that maybe he could ride bareback after all—and perhaps just a tiny little bit like an Indian.

"That's the stuff. Now you've got it!" Sam yelled, as Jerry loped by.

"Gee, this is great," Jerry said, pulling up at last. "Just so's Applesauce doesn't trot."

"Oh, we Indians don't trot much," Sam said. "At a gentle lope like that, old Applesauce can go along for hours. Climb down. You've had enough for one day."

But Jerry was having so much fun now, he hated to

stop. All his life he had wondered what it would be like to race across the plains on a horse, riding free and wild like an Indian. And now, he thought, I think I could do it. "Sam," he asked, "what's it like when the horse *really* runs?"

"Maybe you better wait a day or two until you loosen up," Sam said dubiously.

"Gee, Sam," Jerry said. "I've waited a long time for this. How about letting me run him just once around the haystack?"

"You think you're ready?"

"Sure."

Sam shook his head doubtfully. "All right," he said. "I'll start you off, but take a hard grip on the mane, grip with your knees, and look out when he turns."

"Oh, Applesauce isn't that hot," Jerry said. "I'll hang on."

"O.K., here we go," Sam said. "Get ready."

Jerry gripped with his knees, took a firm hold on the mane, and lifted the reins. Immediately he noticed a change come over Applesauce. He felt the horse's muscles begin to tense. Applesauce pulled his legs up under him. He was getting ready to race.

"On your mark," Sam said.

Jerry felt his own muscles tighten, and he saw Applesauce raise his head and cock his ears.

"Get set."

Jerry leaned forward just a little. He felt a quiver go

through the horse. This was it. This was how it would be in the race.

"*Go!*"

Applesauce jumped ahead. He exploded like a rocket. Jerry was ready, but it did no good. On the first jump he lost his grip on the mane. By the second jump, Applesauce was at a dead run, and although Jerry was gripping with his knees, he was halfway to the horse's rump. By the third jump he was sitting just over the horse's tail, and Applesauce was so surprised that he kicked up behind.

That loosened Jerry once and for all, and though he grabbed wildly at the horse's back, he slid over the rump and landed on the ground with such a bang that lights seemed to flash everywhere. He saw red fire. He saw white lights. He saw giant Fourth-of-July pin wheels. He gasped for breath, and then everything went black.

CHAPTER THREE

The Imaginary Haystack

"Hey, Jerry! Jerry! You all right?"

Gulping for breath, Jerry opened his eyes. Two faces stared down at him. One was brown with big, black, worried eyes. The other had a long, long nose with rubbery nostrils and hairs sticking out of its chin.

"Whew!" Jerry gasped. "Look! . . . Look! Applesauce is worrying about me."

Applesauce blew on Jerry, his nose making a riffling sound. He didn't know what to make of all this. He nudged Jerry and pushed at him, and Jerry, still breathless, tried to laugh as he slowly clambered to his feet.

"Gosh, did you break anything?" Sam asked, feeling Jerry's arms and legs, worriedly.

"Nope," Jerry said. "Just knocked my wind out. . . . Ouch!" He took a step and it hurt so much, he stopped to rub it gingerly. "I feel as though I'd had one terrible spanking though," he said, groaning.

"You better walk back to the ranch," Sam said. "It'll

hurt, but maybe you won't stiffen up so fast. Take a hot bath and go to bed."

"Yeah," Jerry said, limping around. "Only . . . only. . . ." He stopped. "Say, I can't do that, Sam."

"Why not?"

"If I come limping home leading my horse, the others will begin to ask questions. They'll know I've been up to something. They'll figure us out. Guess the secret. Sam, I've got to ride home!"

"I guess you're right." Sam saddled up the apaloosa, while Jerry walked around trying not to limp. Then, aching in every limb, he crawled into the saddle.

"Ride him with the reins dead," Sam said. "It's bad for Applesauce. But you'll have to pretend that you've got the same old kid pony."

"Don't worry," Jerry said, wincing at every step the horse took. "We won't race like the pony express."

A few minutes later when Jerry rode out of the timber, he saw that his worst fears were justified. They were all there. Garth had just turned his horse loose in the corral. Muriel was unsaddling, and Ted was rubbing his horse's back. Chuck Wallace, the corral boss, watched over them all to make sure they hadn't brought in overheated horses, and, worst of all, Jerry saw his mother waiting for him, sitting on the bench in front of the leather shop. Jerry thought he might fool the kids, he might even get by Chuck's cold blue eyes, but once his mother got a good look at him, he could never fool her.

Jerry rode into the yard as quietly as he could. Applesauce, feeling the reins lying slack against his neck, seemed to forget he was a race horse. He ambled in looking his worst—a kid pony for beginners.

Jerry, moving down to the far end of the saddle house, put as many people between himself and his mother as possible. He almost cried out as he dismounted, but he pulled the saddle off, slipped it over one of the wooden horses in the shed, and led Applesauce to the corral.

He had turned and was almost back at the yard when his high cow-boot heel turned on a pebble, and before he could stop himself, he said, "Ouch!"

"What's the matter?" Jerry's mother rose from the bench. "Jerry! What have you done to yourself?"

As everyone paused and turned toward him, Jerry stopped walking and tried to look like a man without a terrible ache.

"You look pale," Mrs. Phillips went on. "What have you been doing, Jerry, riding too hard?"

Garth giggled. Muriel looked embarrassed, and Chuck smiled slightly.

Jerry was glad when he felt himself begin to blush. At least he wouldn't look pale. But he was afraid to take a step, afraid of limping.

"Yeah, Jerry," Garth said, "you been running that poor horse to death again?"

"I'm all right, Mother," Jerry mumbled, and risked a step toward the gate.

"You're limping," his mother said. "Did you fall off?"

Everybody laughed then—even Muriel, who had been nice to Jerry during those first few days. "Fall off that skate?" Garth asked, slapping his knee. "Dreamy, you didn't!"

Jerry's mother walked over to him, meeting him half-way. He was really limping now. He simply couldn't help it.

"Where have you been?" Ted asked. "Racing your charger all by yourself?"

"Yeah, you training up that old bear bait for the race?" Garth added, laughing.

This was so close to the truth that Jerry didn't know what to answer. He was no liar. But Jerry decided that at least he would make them worm it out of him.

"Well," he said, "what happened wasn't much."

"Come on, Dreamy," Garth said, "out with it."

"I thought I told you kids not to do that," a voice said. Everyone turned. It was Chuck Wallace.

"Do what?" Jerry asked, surprised.

"Slide down haystacks," Chuck said. "It can pull the hay loose. Waste it. You came down too hard, didn't you?"

"No . . . I . . . I . . . ." Jerry didn't know what to say.

"Don't argue," Chuck said. "I know what you done.

Now I'm warnin' all you kids. You stay off them haystacks or I'll put every one of you afoot for a week."

"But we haven't been near a haystack," Garth said. "You mean Jerry went out all alone and slid down—"

"I said no arguments," the corral boss broke in. "Now, Jerry, you go get yourself a hot bath. You're new here, so I won't do nothin', but don't let it happen again."

"Yes, sir," Jerry said, still puzzled. "I won't."

He walked past the others then, and he could see them watching his limp. He could feel their eyes on him as he opened the gate for his mother. A close shave! But Chuck—why had he said that about the haystack? Did he really think I was sliding down haystacks by myself? he wondered. As he passed the corral boss he looked up, straight into the cold blue yes. Then something happened —at least Jerry thought so. He thought he saw Chuck give him just the shadow of a wink.

The next afternoon, Jerry waited until he was sure all the others had left the corral before saddling up and starting for the hayfield. But as he entered the timbered trail he pulled up suddenly. A figure moved like a shadow in front of him, noiselessly appearing from the underbrush. It was Sam.

"Can I hitch a ride?" he asked, smiling gently. "Take your foot out of the stirrup and let me up behind you."

"Gee, you sure travel quietly," Jerry said, letting Sam crawl up behind the cantle of his saddle. "I've often won-

dered if Indians could still move through the woods like that."

"Some of us do," Sam said. "We like to stick to old ways when we can."

They rode along slowly, so as not to tire Applesauce, talking about the Indian days. "This was winter country," Sam said. "The high rimrocks keep off the snow, so that the ranges are bare. In the old days the buffalo drifted up here when the snow covered the flats. And our tribe used to follow them up the river to get meat for the cold months —Wait! Stop, Jerry!" Sam was suddenly tense. "Listen!"

Startled, Jerry pulled up. "I don't hear anything," he said.

"I do. Hoofbeats. We mustn't be seen together. . . . Good-by . . . meet you at the field." Sam dropped from the horse, slid across the trail and into the brush just as Garth, Ted, Muriel, and several others appeared around a corner of the trail.

"There he is!" Garth said as the group reached him. "What are you doing, Jerry, racing your bronc again?"

"I'm looking for Indians," Jerry said, truthfully, watching the brush for any sign of Sam, any branch that moved, anything to show, in broad daylight, where the Indian might be. But Sam had disappeared like a ghost.

"Boy, you sure are getting dreamier and dreamier," Garth said. "Come on, gang. Let's go out and look at where the race track's going to be." Laughing, the rest of them waved to Jerry, and the cavalcade pushed on down

the road toward the ranch pasture. That was a close shave, Jerry thought, watching them disappear. Darn close!

He worked hard with Sam that afternoon, and by dinnertime he felt so tired and stiff that he paid little attention to the others when they giggled at him for always riding alone. He still wished that they wouldn't call him "dreamy," but as he started for his cabin and a long night's sleep, he thought of the reserve power he had felt in Applesauce that afternoon, of the free feeling of riding bareback, and of how fast the apaloosa could neck-rein. Let 'em laugh, he thought. I'll show 'em. And so will Applesauce.

He had just reached his door when his mother called him from her cabin porch. "Jerry, come here a minute. I've got good news for you."

He walked across to her through the dusk. "Dad's coming, Jerry," she said. "He'll fly out and join us in about two weeks. Isn't that wonderful?"

"Gee, that's great!" Jerry said. "Will he be here in time for the races—the O-Mock-See?"

"He certainly will, Jerry. And that reminds me, there's something else I want to speak to you about."

Jerry's heart sank. When his mother wanted to "speak to him" about something, it always meant she was unhappy about him.

"Jerry," his mother said, "I understand that you don't play around much with the others, that you don't even go riding with them any more."

"Sure, Mother. I've been riding with them some."

"Well, I think I know what the trouble is," she went on. "Garth's mother says that Garth told her that you have the worst horse on the ranch."

"Gee, that's not true, Mother," Jerry said hastily. "Applesauce is a good horse. I like him, and he's teaching me a lot."

"I've seen you, Jerry," his mother went on. "You come in all by yourself. That old horse can hardly move, and you know it."

Jerry's heart sank all the way to his boots. "But he moves faster than you think," Jerry said. "To tell you the truth. . . ."

He stopped. Surely he could tell his own mother the secret. She was kind of proud of him when he did things well. But she got excited and sometimes she talked about him. If Garth's mother found out what was going on, Garth would hear about it. If Garth heard, he would ride bareback, too, and . . . and. . . .

"What were you saying, Jerry?"

"The truth is I don't want another horse, yet, Mother. I want to learn more from this one."

"Well, I'm sorry to disagree with you, Jerry," his mother said, "but you know perfectly well that Garth has ridden all his life. His family have a lot of money. They own horses in the East. Why, Garth even plays polo. He knows what he's talking about, Jerry, and I think you should have another horse and ride more with the other boys and girls."

"Garth doesn't know so much," Jerry grunted. "He's not a cowboy or an Indian."

"Just the same, Jerry, you should have a good horse. Your Dad and I brought you out here so you could learn to ride, and you'll never learn on that old skate. As a matter of fact. . . ." She paused.

Suddenly, Jerry knew what she would say next. He didn't want to hear it. He wanted to stick his fingers in his ears, run away, do anything but listen to his mother's next words.

"As a matter of fact, I've spoken to that nice corral boss, Mr. Wallace. He told me he would give you a better horse as soon as possible."

CHAPTER FOUR

Sam Disappears

Jerry knew that if Chuck changed his horse there was nothing he could do, because at the corrals Chuck's word was law. And he would just have to go on being a tenderfoot on a dude ranch. He'd have to ride with the others behind Garth and have no chance to win a race.

The next morning when he finally went down to the corrals, he watched Chuck carefully, waiting for the blow to fall. Nothing happened, and he rode to his secret meeting with Sam as usual.

"Perhaps he will do nothing," Sam said. "He knows you like the horse."

"I don't know what I'd do if I lost Applesauce," Jerry said. "Without you and Applesauce, the ranch wouldn't be much fun. Gee, you're getting to be almost like a brother."

Sam looked at the ground, scraped one foot in the

dust, and glanced up suddenly. "You want to be my brother?" he asked.

Jerry realized that Sam was serious. He had asked a question he thought very important.

"You bet, Sam," he said. "I sure wish I were."

"There is a way." Sam's face had no expression. He looked very Indian, Jerry thought. "You could be my blood brother. It is an old custom in my tribe. . . . If you want. . . ."

"All right," Jerry said. "Yes. It would be wonderful."

"We must cut our wrists and mix the blood," Sam went on. "It is the ceremony of keeping word. And very important to us."

"Can we do it right here, right now?" Jerry asked.

"Yes." Sam gazed steadily at Jerry. "If you're sure."

Jerry felt a warmth in him, a great affection. Here was a real Indian and he wanted a brother. "I'm sure," he said. "Have you got a knife?"

"Yes," Sam pulled a jackknife from his pocket and opened it. Jerry saw the long, sharp blade. He thought of the danger of cutting his wrist. He felt his heart start to thump. Would Sam know how to do it?

Jerry knew he could say nothing. He would have to trust Sam not to cut too deep, not to hurt him too much.

Sam gazed at the blade in his hand, turning it over slowly. Then he looked up, a troubled expression on his face. "This is a big knife," he said. "I wonder. . . ."

"Does it have to be the wrists?" Jerry asked, his voice just a little bit shaky as he watched the blade gleaming in the sun.

"No." Sam shook his head. "We have no special ceremony for it. It's just that we must mix the blood. . . ." Suddenly his face lit up. "Is that a trout fly in your hat?"

"Sure."

"Then let's use that. Brothers must not endanger each other's lives."

Jerry, heaving a sigh of relief, took off his hat and unhooked the royal coachman sticking in the brim. "We can just prick the ends of our fingers," he said.

"And we will take no chances with them," Sam added. "We'll purify the steel first." Reaching into his pocket he pulled out a big wooden kitchen match. "Good thing I'm the chore boy," he said, "and must light the incinerator sometimes." He took the fly from Jerry and scratched the match on the seat of his pants. Then, holding the fly carefully by the feathers, he let the match burn under the barbed hook.

"Good," Jerry said, thinking of how his mother worried about germs.

"Now hold out the left hand," Sam said. Jerry held out his left forefinger and Sam pricked it lightly, then immediately pricked his own finger as well. As the two drops of blood oozed forth, he added, "Now raise your right hand." Both boys raised their hands high, as Indians do, and rubbed the two fingers of their left hands until the two drops of blood mixed. Then they lowered their right hands and gripped them in friendship.

"Now repeat after me," Sam said. "You and I, Sam and Jerry, have joined our blood in secret." Jerry repeated it, feeling close to Sam and more like an Indian than ever before. "We have joined as brothers in the ceremony of keeping word." Jerry said it after him. "And from now on, our blood is mixed. We are joined forever as brothers by the sacred ritual of keeping word."

Jerry felt the strong hand grip his. He gripped back as hard as he could, and for a moment neither spoke. Then suddenly Sam grinned. "Good, my brother," he said. "Now get on that horse. We've got work to do."

The days passed and Chuck gave no sign of changing his horse. Jerry almost forgot about it until one day, about a week later, he arrived at the corrals with a book for Sam, about how the Nez Percé Indians bred apaloosas. As Jerry leaned on the fence that morning to watch the wranglers catch up horses, he saw Garth brushing the bay's back, and he couldn't help admiring the big-muscled, chunky horse that made Applesauce look so small and rangy. Muriel was combing the little sorrel's mane to make it shine in the sun, and after returning the currycomb to its box, she noticed Jerry standing in the background.

"Hey, Jerry," she said, "we're riding down to Rock Creek. Come on along."

"No thanks," Jerry said. "I've got some other things to do." He kind of wished he could go. He liked Muriel and some of the others, even if he didn't get along well with Garth. But Applesauce mustn't go dude-riding. He had real work to do.

"Oh, come on," Ted Jackson said. "Join the gang for once. We'll wait for old Applesauce."

"Sure," Garth said, throwing a saddle blanket across his horse's back. "We've got all day, kid. We'll give Applesauce time to pick some flowers. You can even bring your book and read him some poems." The others laughed at this.

"*You* wouldn't understand 'em if I did," Jerry said. "Applesauce knows more long words than you do."

Jerry got a laugh this time, and Garth dropped his reins and walked over to him. "Who cares on a ranch?" he asked. "What do cowboys care about books. That's dude stuff to us."

"What makes you think you're a cowboy," Jerry said. "You're just a dude like the rest of us."

"Oh, yeah?" The older boy was towering over Jerry now. He had his chin out. "Well, any time you think you can make that skate of yours do anything, come on along. Show me."

"All right," Jerry said. Then he thought of Sam—and his promise.

"All right what?" Garth asked. "Either start something or go off and slide down haystacks by yourself."

"Take it easy," Jerry said, holding himself in. "The summer isn't over yet."

"Backing down, huh?" Garth laughed. "Listen, sonny, before you start talking you better get yourself a horse. That old plug you ride should be shot for bear bait."

"Wait until the races, Garth." It was Muriel trying to come to his rescue. "He hasn't been here but a short time."

Jerry blushed. She was nice, but he could look after himself, and he didn't want them to get the idea that he was waiting for the O-Mock-See. "Oh, go play cowboy, Garth," he said. "I can't help it if Applesauce doesn't seem very fast. Who knows? Maybe I'll get a new horse."

A second later Jerry realized his mistake. Chuck Wallace, who had just finished saddling a mare for one of the older dudes, turned and said, "That reminds me, Jerry, how would you like a new horse right now?"

"Why, I . . . I . . . guess so. . . ." Jerry realized the blow had fallen.

"I've got a new dude kid coming tomorrow. I can give him Applesauce. Tell the boys at the corral to give you Sugarfoot."

"Gee, that's wonderful!" Muriel said, jumping up and down with delight. "That's the little black mare with the four white feet. She's got lots of pep, Jerry. You'll keep up well with her."

"Sure," Ted said. "You'll do fine on Sugarfoot."

"She's not so bad," Garth added. She can't catch Big Bay. But at least you'd learn something on her."

They were all watching him, waiting to see his reaction. He could feel Chuck's eyes boring into him, and for a moment he couldn't even think. If he said no, they'd all take him for a sissy. Once he said yes, he would have lost Applesauce forever. Sugarfoot was a lively little mare who shied at bits of paper and ran with her head up and her ears forward. She was fun . . . but she could never catch Applesauce—not if he rode bareback like an Indian.

"I guess not today, thanks," he said to Chuck. Maybe he could put it off long enough to think of something. "I . . . I guess I don't want to ride."

He saw the light go out of Muriel's face. He saw Garth smile as he mounted his bay, and he saw Chuck shrug and turn away to saddle another horse, which made him feel that Chuck had no more use for him.

"Gee," Muriel said, staring at him. "That was a wonderful chance . . . and you missed it."

"Go read your book, Dreamy," Garth said. "Come on, you guys." He waved his arm like a cavalry officer signaling, forward. "Let's get going."

Shaking their heads in surprise, the others mounted their horses and followed Garth through the ranch gate.

Jerry was so angry, so hurt, and so worried about losing Applesauce that his eyes stung and there was a lump in his throat. He even felt like crying.

As the yard emptied, he stumbled into the dark saddle house, where the saddles lay on long wooden horses, and he walked to the far end of the building to where his saddle and bridle were lying. He put his hand on the horn, felt the bridle and the bit that went into Applesauce's mouth, and he gritted his teeth while he fought to control himself.

At home and at school he was part of the gang, he thought. He could be part of it here, right now, if he had given up Applesauce and taken Sugarfoot. What was the use of all the secrecy? Why not admit he was riding like an Indian? Maybe he could get Sam into the gang, too, when he wasn't working. And so what if he didn't win the race?

The only thing was that he had promised Sam, his secret blood brother. If he told Sam now that he didn't want to go on, what would the Indian boy think. . . ? But then, he had probably lost Applesauce anyway. And suddenly he thought of the horse following him from the corral, bunting him in the back of the neck with his soft, mushy nose—

"Whatcha doin' back *there*?" a voice asked.

Jerry looked up from the bit he was fondling and saw, standing in the doorway, silhouetted against the bright sunlight, the lanky figure of Chuck Wallace.

"I . . . I don't know," he said, weakly.

"Well, what's the sense of it then?" Chuck leaned comfortably against the doorframe.

"I . . . I . . . I'm darned if I know that either," Jerry said, trying to laugh.

There was a long pause. Jerry wished he could think

of something to say that made some sense. He felt like a fool. Or maybe like a worm. He wanted to squirm out of there, to get away from the cold eyes he knew were on him.

"Didn't I see you feedin' that old apaloosa oats yesterday?" Chuck asked at last.

"Yes," Jerry felt he must say something, so he started blurting words out, fast, crazily. "Yes, I'm feeding him oats to give him more pep. He's really a good horse. He's an Indian horse, you know. He has a real Indian brand on his shoulder, and Sam says that he's a good horse and . . . gee, I like him," he ended lamely.

"Been duded too much," Chuck said.

"I know . . . ," Jerry rushed on. "But he's getting better and . . . by the time that. . . ." He almost added something about the race, then remembered his word to Sam. "Well, anyway, he's getting better and, gee, Chuck, can I keep him?"

Jerry held his breath. He realized suddenly that this was his chance, his only chance to save Applesauce.

"Sugarfoot's got more life," Chuck said.

"Yes, she has," Jerry said. "But . . . but . . . Applesauce is a kind of a pet, and, oh, gee, Chuck, I sure'd like to go on riding him."

Chuck took a cigarette paper and a package of tobacco from his pocket, rolled a cigarette neatly with one hand, and lit it.

"I need him for this raw dude kid coming tomorrow,"

he said, blowing a drift of blue smoke into the sunlight. "He's safe."

"But . . . but. . . ." Jerry saw all his hopes disappearing like cigarette smoke in the sun. It was over. He had done his best.

"And your mother said you should have a new horse," Chuck went on.

"But Mother doesn't understand. She. . . ." Jerry couldn't think of anything more to say except, "Aw, gee, Chuck. . . ."

There was another pause. Then Jerry heard horses' hoofs, which meant that dudes were returning from a ride. Chuck would leave to help them unsaddle, to talk to them —and it would be too late. He saw Chuck toss away the cigarette, stand free from the saddle-house doorway, and wave to the oncoming riders. He started to leave. Then for just a second he paused, turned, and with his face hidden in the shadows, he leaned back into the saddle house. "O.K., kid," he said. "You keep him."

Later that afternoon at the hidden hayfield, a jubilant Jerry asked Sam about Chuck Wallace. "Do you think he's on to us?" he asked. "Does he know what we're up to?"

"I don't know," Sam said, scratching his black hair. "Maybe he does. But he's a good guy. If he is on to us, I don't think he'll talk."

For the next hour, Jerry practiced fast starts. Sitting

up there waiting for Sam to say "Go!" he wasn't scared any more. He could feel his balance on the horse's back. He knew that when old Applesauce pulled his legs up under him and made his muscles go tense, he'd be able to stay on—grab the mane, grip with his knees, but stay on. And as Applesauce rocketed ahead as though shot from a gun, Jerry knew he was right to keep his promise and to wait for the race, no matter what the others said and thought of him.

The next afternoon, Jerry wandered down to the saddle house as usual. It was all very well to run a horse in secret, he thought. But when Sam was off helping the irrigator or doing some other job, he found himself getting pretty lonesome. He avoided the corrals until the others had gone riding, but horses drew him, and he often spent time gazing at the ranch "cavy."

"Hi," a voice said behind him, as he leaned on the corral fence.

He turned and saw Muriel walking up behind him. "Gee," he said, "why aren't you out riding?"

Muriel blushed under her deep tan and shook her head. "Brought my horse in hot and Chuck put me afoot," she said.

"Practicing for the race?" Jerry asked.

"Yes," Muriel said. "I made a mistake. I tried to race Garth. He won by a mile. My horse got hotter than his and I got caught. Gee, I wish somebody had a horse that could give Garth's bay a run for his money."

"Maybe somebody has," Jerry said.

"Not a chance," Muriel sighed. "And I sure get tired of being bossed around by him. He thinks he knows everything. If I just knew how to fish, I'd forget riding for a while and go after some trout."

Jerry looked at his watch. He had an hour and a half to wait before meeting Sam at the hayfield. "Let's go," he said. "Maybe I can find you one."

Jerry got his rod and net, and, with Muriel trailing behind him, he took her to the mouth of Spring Creek where the brook swirled into a big hole as it entered the main river. It was a good spot for big ones, he knew, and it was near enough to the ranch so that he could get back in time to meet Sam. The water was just a little milky, he thought, because thunderstorms in the mountains had started distant landslides way up at the headwaters. He wanted a fly with glitter, and he tied a Wickham's fancy to the leader because it had a shiny body.

"You better practice a little first," he said, showing her how to get a cast out, how to bend her wrist, and how to avoid catching her fly in a tree.

Muriel practiced on shallow water, and Jerry was delighted to see how fast she learned. She was naturally graceful, her wrist was limber, and she was soon putting out quite a long line.

"Gee, this is fun, Jerry," she said.

Jerry thought so, too. He forgot to be lonely, and, as all good fishermen do, he became lost in the sport and thought of nothing else—not even of Garth and Sam and the horse race.

"Now you're ready," Jerry said at last. "The sun's bright, and you'll have to cast from way back. Drop your fly in that hole there, where the water is deep and swirls around. I think there are some big ones in there."

Muriel became very tense. Her eyes sparkled as she crept up toward the bank. She cast as deftly as she could, but her backcast caught in a willow behind her, and she had to wait while Jerry unhooked the fly from a branch. "Take your time," he said. "You'll get there."

Her next cast was short and hit the sunlit rocks on the near edge of the bank. "Darn!" She brought in her line. "I'll never do it, Jerry, never," she said, in a low voice as though the fish might hear her.

"Just a little more line." Jerry found himself whispering, too. "Don't get excited."

A beaver in the dam up the creek plopped into the water with a splash. A woodpecker hammered on a distant tree, and the brook, racing toward the river, gurgled as it swished into the deep trout hole. Muriel cast again, and this time the little green fly landed in the water.

"Hold it," Jerry murmured. "Let it go downstream."

The fly swirled in the water, going round and round. Then suddenly it disappeared. Muriel's rod bowed almost double.

"Jerry . . . Jerry!" she shouted. "I've got him. What do I do now? What do I *do*?"

"Hold the tip up," Jerry yelled. "Hold it high."

Muriel was so excited that she kept shouting "Now what? Now what?" But she kept the tip up. And instinctively, she began to play the fish toward the shore.

"That's it," Jerry said. "Don't hurry. Keep the tip up and, when you get a chance, reel in a little. Work him toward the sloping bank."

Jerry unhooked the net from his belt, as Muriel backed up. "When you get him in shallow water, let me net him for you," he said.

"Oh no, Jerry. Let me do it myself." Muriel held the rod with one hand and reached wildly toward him with the other for the net.

"O.K.," Jerry said, laughing. "But don't hurry." He passed the net to her, and she began to work the fish into shallow water. "Now, now I'll get you," she said to the fish as it swirled into view. "Oh, what a beauty."

"Easy. Wait till he's tired," Jerry warned. But it was too late. In her hurry to get the trout, she rushed to the water's edge and scooped wildly with the net. She missed and, throwing herself off balance, fell headlong into the water.

Jerry rushed in after her. He saw a hand with the rod in it, then a blond, wet head and Muriel's face. He plunged in to help her, but she waved the rod wildly at him. "The fish!" she yelled. "Never mind me. Grab the rod."

Jerry took the rod, and she clambered to her feet, still waist-deep in water. "Oh, Jerry, did I lose him?"

Jerry reeled in and felt the line tug. "No, he's still there," he said. "Can you find the net?"

"Oh, yes." Muriel plunged around in the water, recovered the net, and, grabbing the rod from Jerry, played the fish toward the shore once more. This time the fish seemed to give up. It was beginner's luck, Jerry thought, as he saw the streaming Muriel reach down with the net and bag the trout.

"Oh, boy, isn't he a beauty," she said, holding up what Jerry thought must be a two-pounder. Her face still glowed with excitement. "Gee, Jerry, that was fun. Thanks a lot." She waved the fish around happily. "I wonder if I could get my picture taken with it," she said. "Don't you always have your picture taken with a big fish?"

"Not when you're that wet," Jerry said. "Couldn't tell you apart."

Just then, while he was unhooking the trout for her, Jerry heard a sound in the willows behind him. Looking around, he saw a face staring at him—a brown face with sad black eyes. "Sam," he said. "Hey, Sam, look at the trout Muriel caught."

For a moment the face stared back at him. The eyes were hurt, the expression almost tragic. Then the face disappeared.

"Sam! Hey, Sam!" Jerry yelled. "Come back. I'll be right with you." Jerry glanced at his watch. Four-thirty! He had been so absorbed in fishing that he was an hour late for his date at the hidden hayfield. "Hey, Sam, wait. I'll be with you in a minute," he called. But no sound came from the willows. The Indian had faded silently into the timber.

As soon as Jerry got back to the corrals he made an excuse to Muriel, saddled up Applesauce, and raced to the hayfield. But no one was there. No Indian glided out of the woods with a shy smile of welcome. Sam was hurt. Sam had selected him, Jerry, to represent the Indians on an Indian horse for the race. They had even become blood brothers. And now Jerry had let him down—had *forgotten* the whole thing to go fishing with a girl.

Jerry hunted the ranch for Sam that evening. He went to the bunkhouse, the cow barn, the wrangle-horse barn, the blacksmith shop. He searched everywhere—and at last he realized what had happened.

Sam was through with him.

CHAPTER FIVE

Corral Trouble

That night, as he lay in his bed, Jerry listened as lightning speared the peaks and thunder crashed from rim to rim across the valley. The rain poured down on the cabin roof, while cottonwood limbs plucked at the windows and the wind sent broken twigs scuttling across the porch.

Jerry tossed and turned and wondered where Sam had gone. Could he have been so hurt that he had left the ranch entirely? Was he hiding from the storm, shivering and cold, under a tree in some distant basin? Jerry realized now how serious it was to join in a ritual like "keeping word." The Indian meant more than the race, more than the secret, even more than Applesauce. He was a true friend, a brother, who had been hurt.

Gradually the storm died and the wind dropped. Distant thunder still rumbled in the canyons, but the clouds drifted away and a moon rose, sending a pale, cold light through the window.

It must have been almost midnight when he heard a

faint tapping sound. At first he thought it might be a tree branch scratching the wall. But when he heard it again, he climbed out of bed and opened the door. The cottonwoods shone silver in the moonlight, and he could see the white patches of snow glistening on the sharp mountain peaks. Then, as he looked around, he saw a dark form at the corner of the cabin, and a soft voice said, "Here! Here are the books you gave me."

"Sam!" Jerry said. "I've been looking everywhere for you. Come in."

"No," Sam said. "Here are your books."

"Gee, Sam, I don't want them back yet. Come in. I want to talk to you."

Reluctantly, Sam moved a little closer until Jerry could see the black hair over his eyes. "I think the Indian and the white man don't get along after all," Sam said. "I thought that we were brothers. I thought you wanted to race an Indian horse. . . ."

"Oh, Sam, I'm sorry," Jerry said desperately. "Muriel asked me to take her fishing. She caught one . . . and fell in the water, and it took longer than I thought and. . . ."

"I know," Sam said.

Jerry decided that he would have to do something quickly. "Look," he said, dragging Sam by the sleeve. "You come in here. Don't you talk about white men and Indians and all that stuff." Jerry pulled Sam into the room, closed the door, and turned on the light.

"Lots of times white people don't like Indians," Sam said. "I thought you were different . . . but now I think you are like the others." He sat on a chair with his head down. "It's the same a lot of places," he went on. "My dad, a real chief, can't go into some hotels and restaurants. Many white men look down on him . . . even if he does race horses and win lots of times. . . ."

Jerry began to understand. Sam was lonesome. He felt left out. He wanted to play around with the other boys and girls on the ranch. And on top of that, he, Jerry, Sam's one white friend, had forgotten—forgotten he was riding for the Indians.

"Sam," Jerry put his hand on Sam's knee. "I know I was late to meet you this afternoon. That was very wrong of me. But . . . but, Sam. . . ." Jerry almost wanted to cry. "We're brothers, remember? We're blood brothers. And no matter how you feel, I'm keeping word. I'm going to try to win that race, even if you never speak to me again. I'm going to ride that horse bareback. I'm going to ride for you and your dad and for the Indians on an Indian horse." Jerry looked as hard as he could into Sam's eyes. "Sam, I mean it!"

At last Sam looked up. He cocked his head like a robin, and his black eyes began to shine. "You *really* mean it? You won't forget again?" he asked.

"Cross my heart and hope to die!"

"Good!" A slow smile curved Sam's lips. "Because, my brother, other Indians will see the race."

"What do you mean?"

"The ranch has asked some of our tribe to come up here the day of the race. At night there will be a big bonfire. The Indians will dance some of the old dances. My grandfather, the old chief, is coming. I have written him."

"Gee!" Jerry was excited now. "Does he know about Applesauce and everything?"

"He knows. He comes to see the white boy who rides for the Indians."

"Oh, Sam," Jerry was almost afraid. "Do you think I can do it?"

Sam got up, opened the door, and stood in the entrance. "Maybe," he said. "But when an Indian is doing important things—like when he is racing his pony—at all times like that—he has to forget about the squaws. At such times, the women have nothing to say." Then Sam disappeared into the darkness. For a moment Jerry tried to watch him go, but he faded into the shadows like a phantom.

The next afternoon, Jerry and Applesauce arrived on the minute and Sam, looking happy again, was waiting for them.

Several days went by, and Jerry not only worked on Applesauce, he tried to work on Sam, too. He wanted Sam to mix with the others. He hoped that he would get to know Muriel so that he could see how nice a "squaw" could be. Once in a while Sam would appear in the evening to see horseshoe pitching if a large group was there, but he always remained in the background, watching the game without expression.

Then one evening after supper they decided on a softball game. The sun was already setting behind Crater Mountain, and shadows were crawling up the rimrock, but there was enough light for three innings. "Who'll choose sides?" Garth asked. "I'll be the captain of one."

Nobody wanted to compete with Garth, to face his fast pitching, until at last Jerry said, "Well, you can't be captain of both sides. So I'll take the other."

"A hero!" Garth said. "Jerry, you've been reading baseball stories. O.K. I pick Ted."

"Muriel," Jerry said, because he knew she was a hot second baseman.

"Harry."

"Jake."

By the time Garth had six players and Jerry five, all the available young people were gone. Then, gazing around the group, looking for one more player, Jerry saw Sam standing in the background, watching from the deepening shadows of the cottonwood trees. "Sam," he called. "Hey, Sam, come on and play some ball."

Reluctantly, Sam joined the group. He looked kind of ragged, Jerry thought, in his worn jeans and faded shirt compared to the dude kids who wore loud, multicolored shirts and fancy pants for dinnertime. But his hair was combed and his shoes were shined. "Gee, I'm not much good at this, Jerry," he whispered. "And I'm not a dude."

"Who cares?" Jerry said. "Lots of the wranglers play with us. You've played ball, haven't you?"

"A little. . . . But. . . ."

"Come on, Sam," Muriel said. "We need you."

Sam looked embarrassed. "You're sure nobody'll mind?"

"Of course not." Muriel laughed. "We're lucky to get you. What do you play?"

"Left field, I guess," Sam said. Jerry saw that, though Sam was embarrassed, he was excited; he wanted to play.

"Get out there, then," Jerry said. "Play ball, Garth. The light's going."

Usually Jerry didn't take these pickup games seriously. The light didn't last long enough for a real game, and they only played for something to do until bedtime. But with Sam out there, this game suddenly seemed important. He wanted Sam to forget he was an Indian and to have some fun.

In the first inning, with Jerry pitching, Ted hit a two-bagger, blasting the ball just over Muriel's head. Then Jerry warmed up and struck the next two batters out. He felt he had some control of the game by the time Garth came to bat, and he made Garth foul twice. Then, anxious for the third strike, he decided on a fast one. He poured it in as hard as he could. Garth swung, and a long pop fly rose into the sunset. Jerry turned to watch. It was going into left field. Sam took his time to get under it. He moved easily, surely. The ball dropped into his hands.

Then, for some reason, he bobbled. The ball bounced from his fingers and rolled into some long grass. Sam rushed after it furiously. He scrambled about, picked it up, and fired it in to the catcher. But he was too late. Garth and Ted both scored, making the score two to nothing.

Perhaps it was the suppressed fury of the little Indian, Jerry didn't know, but for some reason the game suddenly became serious to everybody. Garth pitched better than he ever had before, and Jerry struck out three in a row. Sam, when he came to bat, seemed so intense that even the crowd of dudes, sitting along the sidelines, watched him with interest. But he couldn't hit, Jerry saw. He swung beautifully. His coordination was something to watch. But though his bat hissed through the air like a striking snake, he fanned out—twice.

In the second inning, Jerry managed a two-bagger, but no one was able to bring him in. By the end of the third inning, when Jerry's team had the last chance at bat, the score was still two to nothing. Jerry hurried his team, urging them to make the most of the fading light, feeling that somehow they must win the game or Sam would never join them again. The first batter struck out. Then Jake singled, and Garth, feeling that he might be in trouble, started razzing the batters, hoping to rattle them.

Muriel came next. Jerry enjoyed watching her. She strode to the plate in fury, swinging her bat around her head, her hair glowing wild in the sunset. Her bare arms were so slender that they didn't look as though they could hold the bat up, as she stepped into the box. But she talked back to Garth and waved her bat like a club at him. Garth fired one in, hoping to scare her, perhaps, but she leaned into it, blasted it out over third, and reached second, before the ball could be found under a sagebush.

"Sam's up," somebody said. But Sam didn't step into the box. He walked over to Jerry instead.

His lips were a straight line, and he seemed as tense as a bird dog pointing a grouse. "Pinch-hit for me, will you, Jerry?" he asked.

"Gee, no!" Jerry said. "Go in there, boy."

"No, look. This is all my fault," the little Indian whispered. "I bobbled the ball. That's what did it. And I can't seem to hit, either." Jerry had never seen him so excited. "You can hit Garth," Sam went on. "You bat for me."

"Look, Sam," Jerry said. "This isn't the world series. It doesn't matter. It's only a pickup game. Go on in there." It did matter, though, Jerry thought. It was vital to Sam, somehow.

"O.K.," Sam said, turning toward the plate. "You're the captain."

Garth was glad to see Sam step into the box. "Here comes the Indian windmill," he yelled. "Chief Windmill at the bat." Then he pitched a slow one, and Sam swung so hard Jerry could hear the bat whistle.

"Strike one!" called the umpire, Muriel's father.

"Blast him, Sam. Bring us in, boy," Muriel yelled as she took a lead, and Jerry wondered what Sam thought of the squaw on second base.

Next, Garth pitched a slow outside curve. Sam started to swing too soon, then held it up. But it was over the plate. "Strike two!" the umpire called.

"Chief Rusty Gate," Garth yelled, feeling that he had the game in his pocket.

Then, suddenly, Jerry realized what Sam's trouble was. "Step out of the box," Jerry said. "Hold it up." Sam stepped away from the plate. "Sam, did you ever play softball before?" Jerry asked.

Sam shook his head. "Nope. Played hardball," he said sadly.

"Look, Sam," Jerry said. "That's why you bobbled the fly. That's what's the matter with your batting. That's a big soft ball. Garth's feeding you slow ones. And you swing too soon. Wait for 'em, Sam. You've got to wait."

"Hey, the light's going," Garth yelled. "Quit stalling."

Sam nodded grimly and stepped into the box. Garth, anxious to finish the game, decided on a change of pace. He threw a hard one. It came whistling in. If it had been slow, Jerry thought, Sam would have struck too soon again. But he connected. The ball went up. It went out. It went clear over the recreation hall into the tallest grass on the ranch.

Jerry and his team waited on the third-base line as Jake, Muriel, and Sam came trotting in. "The longest hit of the year," Jerry said, slapping Sam on the back. "Report to the Yanks' training camp next spring."

As the crowd grouped around Sam to congratulate him, Garth came off the mound, grumbling to Ted, "It's no fair letting roughnecks play in a dude game. Sam's only a chore boy."

Jerry felt the anger rising in him. "What are you, a bum sport?" he asked.

"Look who's talking." Garth elbowed his way through the group until he towered over Jerry. "Dreamy, as a guy who won't even ride with the gang, don't talk to me about bum sports."

"You got blasted out of the box, and you can't take it," Jerry said. "The guy happens to be a chore boy. So you have to . . . to. . . ." Jerry was so mad he couldn't speak.

"Dreamy, if you weren't so small, I'd bust you one," Garth said. "I'd—"

"You'd what?" It was Sam. He slid in front of Jerry, and his little legs were like springs. His face had no expression, but his fists were clenched. "Maybe this is *my* fight," he said. "*I'm* the chore boy."

"Break it up, you kids." Muriel's father, a big man, moved through the group like a bull buffalo. "Stop this fighting, or I'll tell every parent on this ranch."

The group dissolved, and when Jerry, still angry, looked for Sam, he had faded away into the growing darkness.

When he ambled toward the corrals the next morning, Jerry realized that this was the very height of the dude season. Groups on horseback—men, women, and children—were leaving the corrals for trips into Elk Basin or over Indian Divide, and Chuck was so busy helping to settle the dudes in their saddles that there was a line of people waiting to have their cinches tightened.

"Say, Jerry," Chuck said over his shoulder as he pulled up a latigo strap, "help them ladies saddle up, will you?"

Jerry's eyes widened. Chuck wanted him—a dude—to help. "Sure, you bet," he said, and rushed to get old

Mrs. Bowen's saddle. While she held the pony's reins and patted its nose gingerly as though it were a Siamese kitten, Jerry brushed off its back, then slipped the blanket and saddle on. Reaching under the horse's belly, he grabbed the cinch ring and slipped the latigo strap through it. He tightened it slowly, making the horse grunt. Mrs. Bowen, he knew, would have no sense of balance. If the saddle were loose, she would fall.

Chuck passed them, stopped for a second, and slid his hand under the cinch ring. "O.K.," he said. "Keep working, will you, Jerry? We're busier than a one-eyed dog loose in a meat house."

Jerry saddled horses as fast as he could, and a half hour passed before the last rider left the yard. At last, Chuck said, "Thanks, Jerry. You done a good job."

They squatted against the fence while Chuck rolled a smoke, and Jerry felt almost as though he were a ranch hand instead of a dude. Together they stared down at the corrals, watching the horses without speaking. Then, at the sound of footsteps, Chuck glanced over his shoulder. "Here he comes like a trail boss huntin' water," he grunted.

Jerry saw a large fat man striding through the gate and wearing shiny, Eastern riding boots, Eastern riding pants, a loud Western "stampede" shirt of many colors, and the stiffest, biggest, most ill-fitting ten-gallon hat Jerry had ever seen. "Who's he?" he asked.

"Guy named Whidby," Chuck whispered. "Big boss told me he was mighty important. Give him anything he wants. Spends money, lots of money, and tough to get along with. That usually means trouble."

"Good morning," said Mr. Whidby. "So these are the corrals, huh."

"Yes, Mr. Whidby," Chuck stood up. "That's the dude string in the big corral."

Mr. Whidby squinted through the dust. "Sure are a terrible looking bunch of horses," he said. "Around Long Island, where I live, we'd shoot them and feed them to the dogs."

"They ain't so bad." Chuck's face was expressionless. But Jerry knew Chuck loved every horse he had and that the ranch had the best dude cavy in the West.

"Gee, Mr. Whidby," Jerry said. "Those are good horses. They just don't look fancy because we don't keep them all shined up in a barn."

Mr. Whidby pushed his stiff Stetson back on his head. "Is that so?" he said. "Where are all the cowboys?"

"The wranglers are riding some parties out on day trips," Chuck said.

"Well, I must say the place looks deserted," Mr. Whidby went on. "Of course I came out here to fish. I find they won't be able to get my tackle up here from the railroad station until tomorrow. As a matter of fact, the fishing doesn't look much good anyway. Water's milky."

"That's too bad," Chuck said, although Jerry thought he sounded almost glad about it.

"Yes, it is. I pay out all this money, travel twenty-five hundred miles, and the river's milky. I only have ten days, and they can't get my fishing tackle to me. Half a mind to leave. But what do you do around here when you *don't* fish?"

"Gee, everybody rides," Jerry said. "That's what's fun on a ranch."

Mr. Whidby hitched his belt up a little over his paunch. "Is that so? Why?"

"I don't know. It . . . it just is. . . . Why don't you go riding, Mr. Whidby?"

"Don't know as I'd want to ride on those old skates," Whidby laughed. "But I don't know. . . ."

"Maybe tomorrow," Chuck said. And Jerry felt Chuck's hand pinch his arm. It was a warning. Something was wrong. "It takes a day or two to get used to the altitude, you know."

"Why? Who cares about the altitude?" Whidby tightened his belt this time. He began to look as though he *might* want to ride. And suddenly Jerry realized what the trouble was. All the dude wranglers were out. There was nobody to take raw, fat old Mr. Whidby out riding. Chuck couldn't leave the corrals in case other guests came down. His job was to see that everyone got the right horse.

"You know, I think I will ride," Whidby said. "Those old beaten-up horses ought to be able to hold up a fat man like me for a little while."

"I'm sorry," Chuck said slowly. "My tally book here

from the front office says you wouldn't likely care to ride, so I ain't got nobody here to take you out."

"Why not?" Mr. Whidby frowned. "This *is* a dude ranch isn't it? Good grief! I can't get my fishing tackle, and now you say I can't have a horse or anybody to ride with."

"I can't cut loose now," Chuck said apologetically. "But maybe I could ride a little circle with you late this afternoon."

"Well, my tackle might be here by then," Whidby grunted. "Say," he turned to Jerry. "Why can't you come with me and show me around?"

"Well. . . ." Jerry shuffled his feet in the dust. "I'm not exactly a dude wrangler, Mr. Whidby—"

"I know that!" Mr. Whidby cut in. "I don't need help riding one of those old skates. I just need someone to show me around."

"But I—"

"That settles it," Whidby said, turning to Chuck. "Saddle me up a horse, please."

CHAPTER SIX

Stampede!

"O.K., Mr. Whidby." Jerry saw the slightest smile on Chuck's face. "That's a good idea. I think Jerry here can look after you real good."

Ten minutes later, Jerry and Applesauce led Mr. Whidby out of the yard on Mouse, an old gray gelding with an enormous head. Chuck winked at him as they passed through the gate. "Take it easy," he said. "Don't run them ponies hard over the rocks."

There wasn't much danger of that, Jerry thought, as they crossed the horse ford and ambled down the lane. In fact, although Mr. Whidby kicked and belted Mouse with his heels, the old gray simply hung his head and wandered from side to side.

"This horse is just as bad as he looks," Mr. Whidby said. "I'm all tired out kicking him."

"He isn't so bad," Jerry said. "Wait a minute." He took his knife from his pocket, and pulling up Applesauce next to a cottonwood tree, he cut a small switch from one of the lower branches and passed it to Whidby. "Try this," he said. "Touch him on the flanks."

"Thanks." Mr. Whidby grabbed the switch and slapped Mouse. The old horse lifted his head and broke into quite a decent short trot.

"That's better," Mr. Whidby said grudgingly. He bumped hard at every step the old horse took, but Jerry was surprised to see that he seemed to like it anyway.

They rode on down the road, and Jerry, trying his best to be a good dude wrangler, pointed out places along the river where the water ran deep under the willows and rainbow trout lurked. He told his dude about the trails that climbed in switchbacks over the high rimrocks to the big-game country and what he knew about the elk, moose, and the mountain sheep that lived high up near the glaciers.

When they had turned back toward the ranch at last, and Mouse was picking up his feet at the thought of getting home, Mr. Whidby said, "Well, for a kid that's been here only a few weeks, you're pretty well up on things, aren't you?"

"Oh, gee, I don't know anything," Jerry said. "But I sure like it out here. I. . . ." His voice trailed off as he heard hoofbeats and voices behind him on the road. Looking back he saw Garth and Ted coming up at a fast trot.

"Good grief!" he heard Garth say. "Look who's wrangling dudes."

Hearing horses behind him, old Mouse decided it was time to hurry for the corral. He broke into a trot. Mr.

Whidby pulled hard on the reins and then squeezed himself around in the saddle to look at the two boys riding behind them. "Friends of yours?" he asked Jerry.

"Just guys, dudes on the ranch," Jerry said. He didn't like them riding up close behind like that. It made Mouse nervous. Sometimes the oldest horses would break loose and run when other horses charged up behind them.

Jerry turned. "You want to go by?" he asked.

"Sure, Dreamy," Garth said. "We don't want to ride behind old Applesauce, that's for sure."

"Then go by easy, will you?" Jerry asked. "This is Mr. Whidby's first ride." He glanced at Whidby, who was holding Mouse in but keeping the reins so high that he could never hold the horse if he really wanted to run.

"Listen to the dude wrangler," Ted said.

"Let 'em by," Mr. Whidby grunted, and Jerry could see that he was scared.

"O.K. Here we come!" Garth shouted suddenly, and sticking his spurs into Big Bay, and with Ted behind him, he charged his horse between Jerry and Mr. Whidby. "Whoopee!" Garth leaned up on the saddle swells, and his horse tore down the road. "Good-by, Dreamy!"

Jerry held Applesauce in, although the apaloosa wanted to take after Garth and show that big bay how to run. But Mouse couldn't stand it. He wanted to get back to the corral, too. He wanted a roll and a drink. Suddenly he pulled hard on the reins. Mr. Whidby pulled back, but his hands were so high on the reins that even when he raised them over his head, it wasn't enough. Mouse took the bit in his teeth and lit out with everything he had.

Applesauce tried to open up, too. For a moment Jerry held back. If he ran after Mouse, it would simply be a race and Mouse would run faster than ever. He could see Mr.

Whidby leaving the saddle at every jump. Daylight shone between him and the cantle.

Jerry didn't know what to do. If Mr. Whidby fell off . . . and broke a leg . . . or was dragged . . . and he, Jerry, was to blame. . . .

Jerry suddenly spurred Applesauce and pulled him to the right. Maybe—just maybe—Applesauce was fast enough to circle old Mouse and corner him where a fence came close to the road a quarter of a mile ahead. It might be done—if Mr. Whidby could stay in the saddle that long!

Jerry leaned forward and Applesauce tore off through the sagebrush. Jerry saw Mr. Whidby ahead and off to his left, still pounding the saddle, still trying to pull up. Wind whistled past Jerry's ears. He wished he were riding bareback to get in every ounce of speed, but even with the saddle Applesauce was ripping through the sage and gaining every minute.

It took less time than Jerry thought to pass ahead of Mr. Whidby. Even though Applesauce had to jump the sagebrush and duck around gopher holes, Jerry was able to turn him ahead of Mouse and angle him back to the road. When Mr. Whidby came pounding by, Jerry was loping along easily. He reached over and grabbed the reins close to Mouse's jaw. Gradually he pulled him to a standstill.

"Wow!" Mr. Whidby slumped in the saddle.

"Are you all right?" Jerry asked, anxiously. "Do you want to get off?"

Mr. Whidby didn't answer for a moment. He stood

in the stirrups and felt of his backside. Then he took off his hat and hung it over the pommel. He reached for a handkerchief and wiped his forehead. At last he turned and, to Jerry's surprise, he had a wide grin on his face. "Gee whiz!" he panted. "You were right, son. This horse has more gumption than I thought."

"Well, would you like to get off and rest?" Jerry asked, still worried.

"Get off!" Mr. Whidby put his hat back on and shook his head. "Shucks, no, Jerry. Why I haven't had so much fun in years. That was exciting. Why, that was real cowboying, wasn't it?"

Jerry felt that he could almost fall off Applesauce, he was so surprised. "Yes, Mr. Whidby," he said, breathing a great sigh of relief. "It sure was. Real cowboying."

The next morning, when Jerry went down to the corrals, Garth, Muriel, and some of the others were currying their horses, and Sam was cleaning up in front of the saddle house. Suddenly Chuck came hurrying down from the front office.

"What did you do to that dude, Whidby?" he asked Jerry.

Jerry's heart sank. "Why, nothing. His horse stampeded and—" He stopped. He would have liked to have told Chuck what Garth and Ted had done. It was dangerous to run through like that. Jerry looked at Garth sitting on the fence. If he told, then Garth and Ted would be put afoot. And he, Jerry, would be called a snitcher.

"His horse *stampeded*? I thought he looked hot. But—" Chuck paused, looking puzzled.

"He cold-jawed on the way home," Jerry said. "I cut him off, though. Mr. Whidby didn't *seem* hurt. Gee."

"He isn't," Chuck said. "He's so stiff he had to eat breakfast standing up. But that ain't going to stop him. He wants to start on a week's pack trip, right now!"

"He does? Why?"

"Because you told him about the mountains and the good fishing over on the other side of the divide. But he's got to go now. That means packs, saddles, sleeping bags, food. I've got to get a cook and a guide and a horse wrangler—" Chuck grabbed his bridle and ran for the wrangle-horse corral.

"What do you know about fishing on the other side of the divide, Dreamy?" Garth asked with a laugh.

"I heard about it," Jerry said.

"Trying to show off. Be the big dude wrangler," Garth said.

"Jealous?" Muriel grinned up at Garth from the bench in front of the leather shop. "I heard what you did, trying to stampede Mr. Whidby."

Garth saw Chuck coming, leading a half-broke bronc. "Quiet!" Garth said. "What you going to do—snitch?"

"Now look here, you kids," Chuck said, after he had saddled the bronc and swung into the saddle. "I've got to ride up to Little Boulder Creek and see if I can get Bo

Snyder to wrangle and Joe Sutton to cook for this trip. We've got pack horses to find, horses to shoe, packs to get out. We're going to be plumb busy around here and every darn man I got is out on the trail. So until the wranglers get back, Joe, the irrigator, will catch up your horses, and Sam will be in charge of the corral."

Jerry saw a stir among the children. Garth sneered and giggled. Sam looked worried.

"Sam is an Indian," Chuck went on. "He knows more about horses than all of you put together will ever know. He's a top hand. And while I'm gone he's the *boss*. Get it?" The children nodded. "He'll keep tally on you," Chuck added. "If a horse comes in beat up, he'll know it. He's got to report it to me whether he wants to or not. So ride easy!"

As he turned his horse, it started to buck. Its head went down and it snorted in fury, plunging at the earth on stiff legs. But Chuck hardly seemed to notice it. He rode as easily as a child on a rocking horse. When the bronc began to tire, he pulled its head up. "So long, kids. Stay in the saddle," he said, and loped off, leaving Jerry and the rest of them openmouthed in admiration.

After lunch, Jerry had an errand to do for his mother, and he didn't get to the corrals until most of the dudes had started their afternoon rides. Garth and some of his closer friends were just mounting as Jerry arrived.

"I tell you what," Garth said. "Let's practice quick starts for the race."

"Yeah," Ted Jackson said. "We'll go up to the post office, run for the corral, and pull up as fast as we can in front of the barns."

"O.K., let's go." Garth turned his horse.

"Wait a minute." Sam, who had been sweeping out the leather shop, stepped in front of the riders. "I'm sorry, but it's against regulations to do that."

"Why?" Garth asked, gazing down at the little Indian.

"Because," Sam said, looking at the ground and scuffing his feet, "there are kids around and dogs and chickens. You might run 'em down."

"There's no children around, except Dreamy here," Garth said, pointing at Jerry, who was standing by the leather shop. "He can get out of the way."

"Well. . . ." Sam was trying to be nice about it, because he knew that all good wranglers are supposed to keep the ranch guests happy. "There's another reason. It's bad for the horse."

Garth laughed. "That's silly," he said.

"No, it isn't. If you keep riding in and out of the yard, the horses get corral-balky. They even get so sometimes you can't get 'em to leave the yard."

Garth slapped his leg. "That'll be a day," he said. "Come on, Ted, let's get out of here and let Chief Know-It-All go back to his tepee."

Jerry saw Sam's eyes narrow and his muscles tense. But the Indian didn't say anything as the others rode out through the wide ranch gate. Muriel, who had been making a tooled belt in the leather shop, came out and joined them.

"I heard that, Sam," she said. "Don't mind him. He's a spoiled boy."

"I know." Sam's voice was low. "I don't care." But he watched the two riders as they reached the post office. Suddenly they turned their horses. "Here they come," he said.

Jerry had time to note that Garth's big bay didn't start as fast as Applesauce could. Then he saw them tear through the gate, pass the saddle house, and pull up hard in front of the barns. Turning again, they trotted by Sam without even looking at him. "Let's try it once more," Garth said.

"Hey!" Sam called after them. "You can't do that. Chuck wouldn't like it." But they paid no attention.

Jerry looked at Sam, who stood quietly in the middle of the yard watching the two riders, his hands on his hips. "Whatever you want to do, Sam," Jerry said grimly, "count me in."

"Me too!" Muriel was furious. Her color was high under her sunburn. With one hand she pulled at her blond hair, and her other fist was clenched as though she wanted to hit somebody.

"Well," Sam looked around, and suddenly that shy grin came over his dark face. "Thanks! Let's just close 'em out."

CHAPTER SEVEN

Jerry Phillips, Horse Wrangler

The big gate at the entrance of the yard in front of the saddle house was rarely closed, and the three of them had to push hard to make it swing clear of the ground.

"Wait a minute," Sam said. "Wait till they start."

The three of them stood with their hands on the center rail, their arms stiff, and their feet braced. Jerry saw that Sam no longer wore a troubled look. His face was expressionless, blank. He was all Indian now, a sort of tiny brave, Jerry thought, ready for the warpath. On his other side, Muriel was all excitement. Her eyes glittered, and she was breathing fast. She was mad clear through.

Garth and Ted had disappeared behind the post office, evidently planning on a longer start. At last Jerry heard the hoofbeats coming hard, and the two riders came around the post office riding at a full gallop.

"Hold it!" Sam said coolly. "Let 'em come. All right . . . one . . . two . . . three . . . *pull!*" Jerry pulled as hard as he could. The gate swung shut in front of the two riders while they still had about 50 feet to go. They pulled up hard, and Garth's horse stopped within a foot or two of the gate poles.

"Hey!" Garth yelled. "What do you think you're doing?"

"I told you not to run your horse in here," Sam said, slipping the big hook into the iron eye that kept the gate closed.

"And I tell you to open that gate." Garth's face was a fiery red as he dismounted his horse. He was a big, tough kid, Jerry thought, bigger than any of them.

"I'm sorry," Sam said evenly. "But right now, I'm the boss."

"Well, let's see you stop me from opening the gate, then," Garth said, swarming up the fence and dropping down on the near side.

Sam stood with his hand holding the hook down as Garth walked up and towered over him. Sam didn't flinch. His face was still blank.

"I'll get you fired," Garth said. "You'll be off this ranch by tomorrow morning, Chief Swelled Head."

Jerry couldn't stand it. He knew that Garth's family had a big house they were renting for the summer. They were valuable dudes. Garth could make it tough for Sam.

Jerry stepped in front of Sam and pushed him gently aside. "You won't fire anybody," he said.

"Well," Garth laughed. "If it isn't Dreamy. . . . Get out of my way, or I'll mop up this corral with you."

"You'll have to fight me, too," Muriel said, pulling at Garth's sleeve. "You'll have to fight me."

Garth shook off her hand. "Girls keep out," he said. Then he reached for Jerry and tried to push him out of the way.

He was bigger and he was stronger. Jerry felt himself stagger. He grabbed Garth by the arms and tried to hold on, but Garth pulled his right hand free, clenched his fist, and slugged as hard as he could. He aimed for the face but was off balance and hit Jerry in the shoulder, sending him flat on his back in the dust.

Jerry scrambled to his feet and was about to tear in with both fists clenched, when he heard horse hoofs coming at a full gallop.

All of them seemed to freeze for a moment like statues. Garth and Jerry were poised to fight. Sam, watching Ted climb the fence, was ready to hold him off. Muriel was so angry she didn't know what to do and stood with her little fists clenched in fury. But all of them looked toward the post office as a rider loped around the end of the porch.

"It's Chuck," Sam said, coming to life. "Get that gate open." He lifted the hook, and all of them, forgetting the quarrel, pushed the gate wide just as Chuck pulled up.

Jerry wondered what Chuck would think of them, all on the verge of a fight, but Chuck didn't even notice.

"Any wranglers back?" he asked. "I need help."

"Everybody's out," Sam said. "What's the trouble?"

"I got Joe Sutton to wrangle horses for the trip," Chuck

said, "but Bo's down at the road camp and they ain't got a phone. It's going to be darn near impossible to get this trip off by tomorrow morning."

"Can't we help?" Jerry asked.

"You sure can." Chuck looked pleased. "But you'll have to take orders. Be real ranch hands."

"Count us in," Garth said. "I think I can be useful."

"O.K." Chuck dismounted and let the bronc head for the corral, trailing his reins. "You got a car, haven't you?"

"Sure," said Garth.

"Do you know how to drive?"

"Yeah." Garth was excited at the chance of driving for the ranch. "You bet I can. I'm not old enough for a license, but—"

"That's all right. This is an emergency, and you'll be on ranch land all the way. Drive down to the road camp. Tell Bo we need him now, pronto. He'll come. Now, Sam, you and I'll get out the pack saddles, bedrolls, tents, and stuff from the storeroom. . . . Jerry, is your horse fresh?"

"Sure." Jerry felt his heart start to beat fast.

"Get him. Do you know the old Smith place?"

"Yes, I rode through there a couple of weeks ago."

"Good. There are ten pack horses in the field there. Get 'em. Haze 'em up here as fast as you can, so we can fit the packs."

"Let me do that," Garth said. "Dreamy can't ride. Let me go."

"You have the car, don't you?" Chuck said.

"Yeah, but Dreamy can't ride well enough to—"

"Maybe he rides better than you think he does. I know who can ride around here. Do you want some help, Jerry?"

Jerry saw that Muriel was still standing in the corral, feeling left out as the others got their jobs assigned to them. "Let Muriel help me," he said, and he grinned at Garth. "She rides well, too."

"Fine. Get going," Chuck said

"Come on, Muriel," Jerry yelled, and broke for the corral.

He had Applesauce bridled and saddled and had vaulted into the saddle before he took time to look at Muriel again. She was right behind him and was watching him curiously. He grinned at her. "Hurry up," he said, and was past the post office before she could catch up with him. As he crossed the horse ford, he broke the apaloosa into a lope. He hoped she wouldn't be left behind, but he had work to do—horse wrangling.

But Muriel pulled up alongside him as they turned off on the road that led to the river bar and the Smith homestead.

"What have you done to that horse?" she yelled. "He goes like a dream."

"Sure!" Jerry grinned at her. "He's real dreamy, like his rider."

Muriel didn't speak again, but she watched Jerry ride.

She kept looking at Applesauce loping along, ears up, head high, just waiting for a chance to really run. Her face was thoughtful as they reached the rocky river bar and had to pull down to a walk.

"Jerry, you've been holding out on me," she said, while their horses picked their way among the boulders. "You've been riding in secret, haven't you?"

Jerry looked at her. She had guessed part of the secret, and he thought that he could tell her everything and she would never talk. But a promise is a promise. "I ride a little," he said, and winked.

"You won't talk, huh?" she asked.

"Nope," he said, sounding a little like Chuck.

On the farther side, they entered a cottonwood grove, and Jerry broke Applesauce into a lope again. It was a winding, twisting trail, and they were forced to ride single file. Applesauce, still ready for a hard run, snorted and pulled on the reins. Then they were out of the grove, passing hayfields. Three minutes later, they arrived at the Smith place.

Jerry pulled up, dismounted, let down the wire gate so that he and Muriel could get through, and then stopped to look for the horses.

The Smith place was an abandoned homestead used by the dude ranch for hay and to pasture extra pack horses. The hay had been cut, and Jerry saw the horses standing at the far end of the field near the old corral. "We'll leave the gate open," Jerry said, "and run the horses through."

It looked easy. The road was there. All they had to do was drive the horses to the ranch.

Jerry and Muriel circled the field and approached the eight or ten horses grazing peacefully. As they drew near, a big hammerheaded red roan raised his head and watched them. He nickered loudly at Applesauce and the sorrel. The other horses' heads came up, and they whinnied, too. Then, as they saw Jerry meant to wrangle them, their tails went up and they stampeded across the field. Jerry and Muriel tore after them, spreading out to drive them through the gate. But just as the bunch reached the break in the fence, the roan, who was leading, stopped dead, snorted at the gate, and then charged on around the field with all the others following him, snorting, kicking, and bucking happily.

"Cut 'em off," Jerry said, turning Applesauce and driving at them again. But these horses had been lying around on rich pasture for weeks. They were fresh, rested, and happy to play games. They crow-hopped and bucked, and when Jerry and Muriel tried to corner them, they waited until the last minute, and then, under the leadership of the roan, they exploded again all over the field.

"Gee, this isn't getting us anywhere," Jerry said at last, pulling up a panting Applesauce.

"My pony's tired," Muriel said, dismounting to give the little sorrel a breather.

"I'm afraid I just haven't ridden enough," Jerry added. "I don't really know the first thing about wrangling horses."

"And Chuck's in a hurry for 'em." Muriel shook her blond curls. "I don't know what to do either."

Jerry leaned on the swells of his saddle and watched the horses. "It's that big old roan," he murmured. "He keeps leading the others."

After their fun and games, the pack horses grazed peacefully again, all except the roan, who had raised his head and was watching the two riders at the other side of the field. His run had made him thirsty. The only available water came from a brook that crossed the corner of the corral. Still watching Jerry and Muriel, he began to ease past the corral gate.

"Look at that," Muriel said. "The roan's going into the old corral."

"Let him get inside," Jerry said in a whisper, as though the horse might hear him and change its mind. "He wants water. When he starts to drink, we'll block him off at the gate."

"What good will that do?" Muriel asked, easing back into her saddle.

"I don't know," Jerry said. "But he's the leader. Maybe we can leave him behind and the others will go along."

"That won't work," Muriel said. "They'll stick by him, won't they? They'll be harder to move than ever."

While they watched, the roan ambled through the corral gate, followed by an old white mare and a brown gelding, with big, work-horse hoofs.

Jerry tensed himself, waiting for them to cross the corral to the brook. Applesauce felt it in the reins, and Jerry smiled as the horse gathered his muscles for a quick start. Old Applesauce was sure doing a job, he thought. He sure knows more about this than I do. If he could talk, I bet he could tell me what to do.

As the roan reached down to drink, Jerry said "Go!"

Applesauce shot ahead and was at the gate in three jumps. The roan's head came up. He spun and rushed the gate, but by the time he got there, the apaloosa was broadside to the entrance.

"Get down and close the gate," Jerry said, excitedly, as Muriel came up. "We've got him!"

While Applesauce stood guard, Muriel got down and pushed the rickety gate closed. "So you've got him," she said, grinning up at Jerry. "Now what are you going to do with him?"

Jerry dismounted and looked through the bars. "I may be wrong," he said. "I sure don't know much about this sort of thing. But he's the leader. I bet if I caught him and rode him and led the bunch, and you drove 'em from behind, we could get all those ponies going."

"But. . . ." Muriel looked worried. "He may not be gentle, Jerry. He might pile you off. You haven't ridden anyone but Applesauce."

"Well, it's time I did," Jerry said. "He must be a pack horse. He can't be a bronc."

"That's what you think," Muriel said. "I saw a pack

outfit leave the ranch last month. Four horses bucked their packs off, and one dude had a hundred-dollar fishing rod broken. Boy, those old pack ponies can get really rough."

"It's the only thing I can think of," Jerry said, unsaddling the apaloosa. "Of course, I may not be able to catch the roan anyway."

Muriel pulled at his arm. "Don't do it, Jerry," she said. "Please don't. You might get hurt, way off here where there's no phone, no doctor."

"Don't look now," Jerry said, "but I've fallen off a horse before." He took the bridle from the apaloosa's head and turned the horse loose. Applesauce nuzzled him a minute, then started cropping the alfalfa growing at his feet.

"O.K.," Muriel said. "But, gee, I wish you wouldn't."

As Jerry began to think about it, he wished he wouldn't, too. The roan was big, with a Roman nose and small eyes. He was an ugly horse and a tough-looking one. Jerry squeezed through the gate and, with his bridle held behind him, approached the animal. His heart was pounding. He was scared clear through, but he felt Muriel watching him from outside the fence, and he knew that he couldn't turn back, even if he wanted to.

The mare and the big-footed gelding moved aside as Jerry approached, and the roan raised his head high. He snorted, he quivered, then he swung around to face Jerry.

He was used to being caught this way, Jerry thought, and that should prove that he was gentle. Jerry moved up on the horse's left side until he could reach the roan's neck. He scratched it and began to talk softly. "That's a good boy," he said. "You've had your fun, haven't you? Now maybe you'll go to work for me, huh?"

The roan's head came down a little, but the whites of his eyes still showed. He quivered as Jerry slowly circled his neck with the bridle reins. "Take it easy, boy," Jerry said. "We need you for a nice pack trip."

At last, Jerry raised the head stall, put the bit in the horse's mouth, and slipped the bridle over the horse's ears. "Good old roan," he said. "Now let's see how you take to a saddle."

Muriel opened the gate for him, and he led the horse through to where his saddle lay on the ground.

"I'll hold him," Muriel said, taking the reins. "He looks as though he might be gentle after all."

"Yeah," Jerry said dubiously, shoving the blanket gently across the horse's back. "I sure hope you're right."

At last, when he had the saddle on tight, he stepped back to see if everything was straight. It looked all right, he thought, except that the saddle seemed to ride high, as though in some way it didn't quite fit. "Looks funny," he said.

Muriel gazed at the horse thoughtfully. "I heard Chuck say once that sometimes a horse gets a hump in his back," she said. "That means he might buck. So Chuck said it was a good idea to lead him around before you mounted."

"That," said Jerry, "sounds like very good advice. You may have saved me a broken leg." He led the horse around the field and was happy to see that the hump disappeared. At last he put the reins around the horse's neck and prepared to mount.

"Keep the near rein tight," Muriel said, "so that he will have to turn toward you."

"Thanks again," Jerry said. "I sure wish right now that I had your riding experience." He could feel his heart start to pound again. This was only the second horse he had ever ridden, and it sure wasn't one assigned by the corral boss, he thought. The roan was showing the whites of his eyes. He was watching every move as Jerry put his foot in the stirrup. Jerry eased into the saddle, got his other foot into the right stirrup, and breathed a sigh of relief. "Now," he said, "here goes." He kicked with his heels.

Nothing happened, except that the horse sort of quivered and heaved. He didn't move his feet. "I bet he's plug," Jerry said. "After all, he is a pack horse." He took the ends of his bridle reins, slapped the horse on each shoulder, and kicked again, hard.

Suddenly the roan reared high, pawed the air, and came down stiff-legged, his head between his knees.

CHAPTER EIGHT

Let 'er Buck!

Right then, Jerry was half out of the saddle. He tried to clutch with his knees, and he made a wild grab for the saddle horn. His whole spine rattled on the next buck. On the third one, he lost his hold on the horn, and then, as the horse tore up the ground, Jerry lost both stirrups. The big roan seemed to shake himself. He plunged again, kicked high behind, twisted like a snake—and Jerry came off. The roan, snorting and blowing happily, pawed the earth and tried to shake the saddle off, too. Then, finding that this was impossible, he stopped dead in his tracks, looked back at Jerry, and began to crop at the grass.

"Are you hurt?" Muriel yelled, running up to Jerry.

"Nope." Jerry struggled to his feet, his face white, his eyes narrowed. He brushed off the seat of his pants, rubbed the back of his neck, kicked some dirt off his boots, and started toward the roan.

"Jerry, you're not going to try again?" Muriel asked, her eyes wide. "Jerry he's too much for you—I mean right now, after Applesauce." She ran in front of him and tried to stop him.

"Get out of my way—" Jerry grunted, then added "please" as an afterthought. He was angry with that horse. He didn't know why. He didn't care. Somehow, some way, that horse, that hammerheaded, wild-eyed plug over there had to be ridden. As Jerry walked up to the roan, it turned toward him, just as it had before, and waited for him to mount.

Jerry took a deep breath and gritted his teeth. Then, holding the near rein tight, he clambered back into the saddle. It hurt. He felt as sore as he had when he fell off Applesauce, and the insides of his legs felt raw from trying to hang on to the saddle.

This time Jerry took a firm hold on the reins with one hand and clung to the saddle horn with the other. Once again he kicked with his heels. The roan tried to bog his head down between his knees, but Jerry pulled hard on the reins. The roan crow-hopped several times, and Jerry hung on to the horn. He knew he looked funny. He was no rodeo rider. But he stayed on top of the horse and the roan, who felt he had had his fun anyway, finally gave up trying to shake off his rider and trotted easily around the field.

"Good for you! Oh, Jerry, that was wonderful." Muriel rode up beside him, her hair flying, her eyes alight.

"Lucky for me he wore himself out," Jerry said, feeling a weariness come over him now that the excitement was over. "Let's get these horses started. Then I'll ride around in front. I'll lead 'em and you drive 'em."

But when they started the horses moving, Jerry was surprised to see Applesauce suddenly come to life. They were headed back to the ranch. His can of oats was long past due, and, by golly, he was going to head home for it.

The other horses, having no other leader, decided that the apaloosa might have the right idea and, stringing out behind him, they followed him like a bunch of sheep.

"Boy, oh boy, look at Applesauce!" Jerry laughed. "He's doing our wrangling for us."

Dusk was settling a few minutes later as they crossed the river bar. The horses plunged into the water, colored yellow by the setting sun. The peaks of the mountains were a burnished copper, and even the snow glaciers resting on the high craters flashed orange in the fading light. Across the range, where the rimrock cut a straight wall for miles, the shadows rose like a curtain, and Jerry, sitting the roan, whistling and slapping his leg to keep the horses moving, felt at last that he was part of it all—a Westerner, a rider, and maybe way down deep, part Indian.

Twenty minutes later, old Applesauce crossed the horse ford in front of the post office at an easy trot. The others followed, with Jerry and Muriel bringing up the rear. Jerry felt tall in the saddle. The roan didn't neck-rein very well, but he carried his head straight out like a cow pony and traveled easily at a jog trot. As they passed the porch, Jerry saw his mother, her eyes wide with surprise, gazing

at him from the doorway. Riding by, he cocked his hat over his eyes, Texas fashion, whistled at the horses and yelled, "Hi, Ma!" then pushed his string on to the corrals.

When they reached the yard, Jerry saw that it was full of men wrestling panniers from the pack shed, pulling out bedrolls, and shaking out the harness on the pack saddles. He found Chuck Wallace checking groceries and yelled, "Where do you want 'em?"

"Leave 'em in the yard." Chuck was in a hurry. "Get halters from Sam at the pack shed and help catch 'em up. Tie 'em to the fence and—" Chuck stopped tightening a cinch and straightened. "Hey," he said, "what do you think you're riding?"

"Well. . . ." Jerry was embarrassed. This sure wasn't a horse Chuck had assigned him. "This horse wouldn't come, so I caught him and rode him."

Chuck put his hands on his hips and looked Jerry over carefully. "You did, huh?" he said. "Did you know he was a bronc? He's no pack horse. I've only ridden him a few times."

"Gee, I didn't know," Jerry mumbled. "I thought he was a pack horse and—"

"Did he buck?"

"Uh-huh."

"Did he pile you off?"

Jerry nodded.

"And you got on him again and rode him out, huh?"

"He didn't buck much the second time," Jerry said.

"I'll be dogged!" Chuck shook his head, and a rare smile crossed his lips. "Well, turn him loose in the wranglers' corral. And help catch 'em up."

He turned back to his horse, and Jerry, after pulling his saddle, led the roan toward the corral. Chuck hadn't said, "Good work," or, "You did well." But Jerry didn't care. He saw that smile and that shake of the head. That was admiration enough from a real cowboy.

As he turned the horse loose, he noticed Garth staring at the big roan. The bigger boy must have heard it all. His eyes were wide with surprise. He didn't say anything, but Jerry had a feeling that Garth would be more suspicious of him than ever now.

By the time Jerry reached the corrals the next afternoon, Applesauce was waiting impatiently, his head hanging over the bars. The pack trip had gone and while loading Mouse with cameras, field glasses, and fishing rods, Mr. Whidby had asked Jerry to go with him. But even a pack trip could not compete with the race—a race only two days away.

Jerry had led Applesauce across the deserted yard, saddled up, and was headed toward the back gate, when he heard horses milling in the wranglers' corral. He pulled up at the corner of the barn and peeked around. Then, amazed, he yanked Applesauce back out of sight. Garth was in the corral, swinging a rope around his head. Jerry had time to see that several of the top wrangle horses were running in circles to keep away from the rope. Three broncs, including the one that he, Jerry, had ridden yesterday, were snorting and plunging and even crashing against the fence.

For a moment, Jerry thought of dismounting and sneaking another look. What was Garth doing in the wranglers' corral? No dude was allowed to fool around the rough string. Most of them were half-broke broncs, still wild and dangerous for dudes. Chuck was still up the river helping to line out the pack outfit, and Garth, knowing it, was up to some mischief. Jerry pondered a minute.

Then he remembered that the race came first. Sam was waiting. Nothing else mattered.

That afternoon Sam had marked off a sort of rough track with pointed sticks. "This is just about the size of the race track," he said. "I heard the wranglers talking about it last night. Kind of sharp turns at each end—and that's good."

"Why?" Jerry asked.

"Because Applesauce turns on a dime, and if you get out in front you can put him on the inside and keep him there. A big horse like Garth's simply runs wider on the turns. It all helps, Jerry. Now, today I want you to run the full quarter mile—just as though you were in the race. I wish I could have sneaked out a pony to pace you, but Chuck would never stand for that."

"He wouldn't like what Garth's doing, stirring up the broncs, either," Jerry said, telling what he had seen in the wranglers' corral. "What do you suppose he was up to?"

"Gee, I don't know." Sam shook his head. "He's kind of like a spoiled bronc himself, I guess. Fights his head all the time. Does the wrong thing. His dad never broke him right."

"He sure isn't nice to you," Jerry said.

"There are lots of people like that about Indians," Sam answered, his face sad for a moment.

Jerry ran Applesauce for a quarter mile. Then Sam criticized him—still too slow on the start, took corners too wide, rode too straight on the horse's back. The sun had set behind the high rimrocks before Jerry put his saddle on again and, hoisting Sam on behind him, started ambling toward the ranch.

Just as they reached the trail entrance at the cottonwood grove, Jerry pulled up short. "What's that?" he asked.

Something moved in the woods, just inside the first line of trees. It was too big for a cow or a deer. Then he noticed the glint of metal from a bit. It had to be a horse.

"I'll bet it's Garth," Jerry whispered. "I'll bet he's followed us."

"Funny he doesn't come out," Sam slipped to the ground. "Let's have a look." He ran toward the woods, but just as he entered, the horse heard him, crashed through the underbrush, burst from the timber, and charged across the meadow. Jerry spun Applesauce and ran after him. He recognized Garth's saddle, with its bright conchos and the long California bit inlaid with silver. But the horse wasn't Big Bay—it was the roan bronc.

CHAPTER NINE

Indian Tracking

Applesauce overtook the bronc in 50 yards, pushed him against the fence, and Jerry reached over and picked up the reins.

As they turned back toward the trail entrance, Applesauce almost pranced, he was so proud of catching the other horse. He blew loudly through his nostrils, and if he thought the bronc he was leading was getting too close, he spun his tail in circles, warning that he would kick if the roan made any trouble.

Jerry found the Indian examining the ground around the trail entrance. "Isn't that Garth's rig?" Sam asked.

"It sure is." Jerry dismounted and tied the bronc to a young tree that would bend if the bronc pulled back suddenly. "That's what Garth was doing. He caught the bronc and tried to ride it."

"And it bucked him off in the timber," Sam said. "He may be hurt. We've got to find him."

"But wouldn't the horse buck him off at the corrals? Maybe he's back at the ranch."

Sam shook his head. "I don't think so," he said. "Sometimes you can ride a horse for several miles before he bucks. And anyway, if Garth got piled in the corrals, the horse wouldn't come out here. He'd stay with the bunch." Sam began examining the ground at the entrance of the trail, working back slowly into the timber. Jerry tried to do the same thing, but a number of horses, including Applesauce, had been over the trail. He could even see where deer tracks had crossed and recrossed the path.

"He came onto the trail here," Sam said suddenly pointing. He was all Indian now, his face intense, his eyes covering the ground an inch at a time.

"How do you know?" Jerry asked. "I can't see anything. Lots of horses have drifted this way since the last rain."

"The bronc is barefooted," Sam said, without looking up. "He's never been shod in his life. Look at those front hoofs. They're worn way short from pounding the range." Sam disappeared in the timber and Jerry, following him, tried to pick up the same tracks. He knew now that he would never be a real Indian, never track game as an Indian could, watching for the the faintest trace.

"That branch," Sam said suddenly. "Look! It's broken. There he is." He stopped tracking and, with Jerry close behind him, ran to where a small branch, about the height of a horse's head, was broken and hanging by a single sliver from a cottonwood.

Garth was there, lying on his back, breathing heavily.

"He's out cold," Sam said. "The branch must have swept him clean off. Lucky he didn't get dragged by the stirrup."

Both boys leaned over Garth, wondering what to do. "Better not move him," Jerry said. "I read somewhere that it's dangerous. He might have a concussion or a fracture or something. What'll we do?"

Sam squatted down and put his hand over Garth's heart, touched his cheek, and began to feel his body to see if there were any broken bones. "Better go back to the ranch, I guess," he said. "We gotta get the nurse. She'll know what to do."

But at that moment, Garth groaned. He moved a little. Then he opened his eyes. "Ouch," he said. "Gee! What. . . ." He looked up, and as his eyes began to focus, he saw Sam leaning over him. "What are you doing here?" he asked. "Where am I, anway?"

"You got bucked off, Garth," Jerry said. "You were riding the roan."

Garth sat up and felt his back tenderly. "Boy!" he said. "That was a fast one. Didn't know what hit me."

"Can you stand up? Any bones broken?" Sam poked at Garth's legs, worrying over him like a mother.

"Sure." Garth got to his feet, winced, rubbed his head and the back of his neck, and bent his knees. Then he turned to Jerry, and some of his old manner came back. "He didn't *buck* me off," he said. "I didn't let him buck much."

Sam smiled. "I know what happened," he said. "You got brushed off under a tree."

"Sure. That's all it was." Garth looked up at the branch. Then the brashness went out of him again. "But I'm sure in a jam now."

"Well, you're not hurt, anyway," Jerry said. "And I caught your horse. Let's get out of here. It's only five minutes to suppertime."

"You're telling me." Suddenly Garth sat down again and rested his back against a tree stump. "Do you know what's going to happen?" he asked. Jerry had never seen Garth unhappy before. All the bully part of him seemed to disappear. He was just a scared kid, Jerry thought, really scared.

"I'm not going to be allowed in the race."

"Why not?" Jerry asked.

"Are you nuts?" Garth said bitterly. "When Chuck finds out I've had a bronc out. . . . I stole him right out of the wranglers' corral. He'll put me afoot for a week. And my family will back him up, too."

"Maybe he won't catch you," Jerry said.

"Look," Garth groaned, "Chuck went out with the pack outfit to keep the horses from turning back. He's back by now. He checks the horses in the wranglers' corral. Boy, he'll miss that bronc in thirty seconds. And the other kids'll know, too. They knew I was going to try to ride him."

"What did you want to ride him for?" Sam asked, suddenly.

"Well. . . ." Garth looked around like a trapped animal. He hated to admit anything. Then he looked up at Sam, and a sickly smile twisted the corners of his mouth. "Well, Jerry rode him. And I thought if even Jerry could ride him, I could."

"Well, sure, of course you could," Jerry said. He understood now. Garth was always trying to prove himself. He really wanted to be best at everything, even if he did have to boast about it afterward.

"Well, I dunno. Anyway, there's another thing." Garth shifted his body against the stump. "I knew you were up to something out here. I thought maybe you had another horse on the quiet. And when I got on the roan, I thought I'd follow you . . . but. . . ." He sighed. "It doesn't matter now. I've goofed up everything."

It was getting dark in the timber. Through the trees Jerry could see deer, does, and little speckled fauns led by big bucks, drifting from the woods into the field. Applesauce whinnied, calling for his oats. Then the ranch dinner bell rang in the distance, clear and cool-sounding against the mountains.

"We're late now," Garth said, pulling himself up stiffly from the tree. "I guess I better go face it."

"Look," Sam said suddenly, "Chuck won't have got back in time to worry about the wrangle stock yet. You get out of here, Garth. Get back to supper. I'll look after it."

Garth glanced for a moment at Sam. Then his face flushed, and he looked at the ground. "What you going to do?" he asked.

Sam stared steadily at Garth. His face was blank. He seemed very Indian there in the dusk, Jerry thought, very quiet and sure of himself.

"I'm an Indian," Sam said. "I can move fast. I can be quiet. I can get that horse into the corral in the dark real easy, and I can keep him from nickering."

"But . . . but. . . ." Garth straightened and looked Sam in the eye. "I haven't been so nice to you, Sam. What do you want to help me for?"

"You've got a race to run day after tomorrow."

That night, Garth and Jerry ambled down to the corrals, pretending they just wanted to see the pigs fed. They found Garth's saddle and bridle on the wooden horse in the saddle house. At the wranglers' corral they saw Chuck pitching extra hay to the broncs.

"Hello, kids," he said. "Ready for the race?"

"You bet," Garth answered.

Sitting on the fence, their boot heels hooked in the corral poles, they watched the ponies awhile.

"Funny about that bronc," Chuck said after a while, pointing to the roan. "Looks like he's been sweating. Not used to a small corral, I guess. Other ponies musta been kicking him around."

The next day—the day before the O-Mock-See—competing horses were kept separate from the dude string so that each rider could brush and curry his mount for the opening parade. The horses must have been surprised at all the sudden attention they received, Jerry thought, watching Muriel shine her horse's hoofs with shoe polish, but they sure did enjoy the thorough back-scratching.

Jerry combed out the apaloosa's mane and tail and brushed the big brown spots until they shone. After a while, Sam joined him and examined Applesauce's feet to make sure that the shoes were tight and that the hoofs had not grown too long.

"Well, I guess he's in as good a shape as he'll ever be," Sam said, backing off and looking at the lean belly. "By golly, his front legs are clean—no bumps or scars." Applesauce, like a spoiled child, ruffled his nose and waved his head at Jerry, asking for more back-brushing. "But he sure is a sissy," Sam said, grinning. "He never got babied like that on the reservation."

"I'm just afraid he won't look dopey enough, now," Jerry said. "He insists on keeping his head *up*. He always wants to run, and I'm afraid he'll look as fast as he is."

"That doesn't matter now," Sam said. "But don't run him in any other events. And don't let on you are going to ride him without a saddle."

"You mean I can't enter the saddle and unsaddle races or any other event at all?"

"I wouldn't," Sam said. "My dad limbers his horses up before a race. But that's all. The quarter mile is *the* big event. And Applesauce *is* old."

"O.K.," Jerry said with a grin. "But even my dad will think I'm nuts. He'll expect me to enter everything."

"But don't tell him!" Sam was suddenly serious. "Remember your promise."

"I don't think he'll talk, Sam." Jerry said.

"All white men talk," Sam snapped. Then he looked embarrassed. "I mean . . . I mean. . . . I didn't mean to say anything about your dad but . . . well . . . your dad just *might* talk to Garth's dad or something."

"O.K.," Jerry said. "I promised, and that's that."

"You promised what?" a voice said. And Jerry turned to see Garth watching them, looking over Applesauce from head to foot.

"I promised to keep a secret," Jerry said.

"Well, you've got one, I guess," Garth said. "I think you have another horse stashed away some place."

Neither Sam nor Jerry said anything at all, and Garth stood awhile, scratching his head. He had something more to say, and he didn't know just how to say it. "You know," he went on, "I . . . I . . . just want to thank you, Sam . . . for what you did yesterday."

"Forget it," Sam said.

"Well . . . I . . ." Garth stumbled on, "I guess

I've been kind of a stinker to you, at that. I'm . . I'm sorry." He turned and started to walk away before Sam could answer. Then, at the corner of the saddle house he turned and some of his old boasting manner returned. "But I'm out to win that race, you guys," he said.

"You know," Sam said, as Garth turned the corner, "he's not a bad guy, at that. And, Jerry, he's going to be tough to beat tomorrow."

CHAPTER TEN

The Race

The next morning dawned hot with the sun beating down on the rimrocks. Dust rose as the wranglers, whistling and slapping their chaps, hazed the dude string down the side hills, across the river, and into the big corral.

"It's wonderful to be out West again," said Jerry's father, who had arrived the night before. "Now let's go down and look at *your* horse."

Jerry knew that he had a hard time ahead. Last night, as he was passing his mother's cabin, he had heard his parents talking earnestly. Although he could not hear what they said, he knew that it was about him—how dreamy he was, how he didn't ride with the gang, and how slow his horse went. His mother didn't realize that at last he was beginning to be popular, that it didn't matter so much if he never rode with the others.

Jerry and his dad leaned on the corral fence and Jerry yelled, "Applesauce!"

Immediately, they heard a whinny. Horses moved aside, and the old apaloosa worked his way through them to the fence.

"Kind of an old skate, isn't he?" his dad asked.

"He's better than he looks," Jerry said quickly. "A lot better. And he sure knows me, doesn't he?"

"Yes, but you should be riding something livelier by now. I understand you refused to change horses, Jerry. Wasn't that a mistake?"

"Gee, no, Dad. I really like old Applesauce."

"Humm."

When his dad made a little "humm" like that, Jerry knew that he was troubled. He had something important he wanted to say and was having a hard time saying it. "You know," his dad went on, "it doesn't hurt to get thrown once in a while, Jerry. You don't have to be afraid."

"I've been thrown, Dad."

"You have? By that old skate?"

"By a bronc." Jerry was glad he could tell something he had done. And he told about the big roan.

"Well, then," his dad went on, when Jerry had finished, "you must be all right. But why don't you ride a real horse all the time?"

"I'll . . . I'll tell you tonight," Jerry said.

"I don't get it." His dad shook his head. "But I guess I can tell this afternoon how well you're doing. You're in this O-Mock-See, aren't you?"

"Yes," Jerry said, wondering how his dad would feel when he didn't enter the various events.

"Well, you know, Jerry"—his dad was being just a little stern with him now—"it cost a lot for us to come out here. We did it for you. You always talked about horses and how you wanted to come West. I had to save for this vacation. I want to make sure it's worth it—or maybe we better go home."

"Yes, Dad," Jerry said. Maybe he wouldn't win the race, he thought. Maybe he wouldn't even place. Anything can happen in a horse race. And he wouldn't have entered anything else, so perhaps . . . perhaps he would have to go East tomorrow . . . and leave Applesauce and the mountains and Sam. Jerry felt his eyes start to burn. He looked up at the peaks shining in the sun, and right then he decided that when he was old enough he would come back and live here. Maybe he'd raise horses. Maybe he'd join the Forest Service. Maybe—

"Let's get back to Mother," his dad said. "We'll see what you've learned about riding this afternoon."

By two o'clock the last preparations had been made. Someone had strung a loudspeaker on a pole above the ranch house, so that recorded music came echoing out to the field where the race track was staked out. The blue jeans and denim shirts of the local ranchers mixed with the bright shirts and Indian-beaded vests of the ranch guests as the crowd lined up along the fence. Across the track at the finish line, Jerry saw what he had been looking for

—Sam stood with three other Indians waiting for the opening parade. Jerry had no trouble identifying Sam's grandfather, who was tall and wore a high-peaked reservation hat. His black hair was braided and hung over his shoulders, and he stood straight as an arrow with his arms folded. "One of the last of the real 'long hairs,' " Jerry thought dreamily, then awoke with a start. "And he's here to see *me* . . . to see me race for the Indians on an Indian pony." And for the first time Jerry felt scared.

They lined up for the grand parade, and as the music broke into a grand march, the procession started. Jerry was amused to see that Garth led, wearing a brilliant blue and yellow shirt and beautiful soft-leather batwing chaps. His saddle shone with silver conchos, and more silver laced his bridle reins. Big Bay, shining like burnished dark copper, wore a martingale and tossed his head and chewed his bit like a stallion. Jerry rode behind him, and he guessed he was a sorry figure compared with Garth. He let old Applesauce plod along, like the Indian horse he was, wearing a split-ear bridle that hardly showed at all. Behind him rode the others, their horses shining and loaded with Mexican silver. Some horses had their tails cut shorter than usual, and Muriel had ten baby-blue ribbons tied to her little sorrel's flowing mane.

The crowd cheered as they paraded around the track, and only the Indians remained silent. As Jerry passed them, Sam yelled, "Hey, cowboy!" The old chief looked at Applesauce gravely, then raised his hand in silent greeting, and

Jerry knew that he was recognized, that the Indians were waiting to see a white boy race for them.

"Ready for the barrel-and-stake race," called Mr. Williamson, the ranch owner, standing in the middle of the field in his bright red shirt. "And first call for the sack race."

Jerry left the group as the others began lining up and rode over to his father and mother, who, he noticed, were sitting next to Garth's parents. He would have to be mighty careful what he said, he thought. He would have to keep his secret until the very last moment. Dismounting, he tied Applesauce to the fence and sat down beside his parents.

"Aren't you in this one?" his dad asked.

"No. I'm going to wait and save my horse," Jerry whispered, looking at Garth's father.

"Yes, I suppose you'd better," his dad said ruefully, watching Applesauce, who was munching grass, his neck hanging over the top of the wire fence. "He doesn't look as though he would last long. . . . But you could have dressed him up a little, Jerry. He looks such a dope."

Jerry saw Garth's father smile at the word "dope." The man was listening all right.

Jerry was surprised at what happened in the barrel-and-stake race. Two barrels were lined up on the field. The contestant had to ride to the first barrel, take out a stake, and drop it into the second barrel. Each rider did it with three stakes, then ran his horse back to the starting line. Although this was done against time, Muriel sped through her trial so fast and her tiny sorrel twisted and turned so speedily that she won with no trouble at all. Jerry noticed something else—Garth was taking it easy on Big Bay. He wasn't going to wear his horse out either.

In the sack race, each boy or girl took a partner. One raced the horse down the field to the other partner and dismounted. Then each one put one foot in a sack and, leading the horse, hobbled back to the starting line. Garth and Muriel won. Garth's parents cheered and laughed, and Jerry, watching his father and mother, saw them try to join in. They were trying to have fun, he thought. But every now and then they would glance at him and Applesauce, and he could see that they felt sad because they thought he was out of it and not one of the gang.

For a moment he was tempted. Should he get into one other race? Just to make them happy . . . ? Then he looked across the field toward the Indians. They were watching politely, he thought, but they weren't interested in sack races. They were waiting, too, waiting for the real thing—the quarter mile. Jerry decided to hang on.

Garth won more events than anyone, and Garth's father jumped up and down, yelling encouragement, slapping Jerry's dad on the back and boasting happily about his son.

Dust rose in a golden haze from the field. People clapped and yelled, and everyone seemed to have a wonderful time, Jerry thought, except his parents. Applesauce cropped the grass dreamily, looking up now and then when the horses ran by or when the crowd applauded the finish of a race. He wasn't worried, Jerry thought, feeling the tension grow in himself. He wished his parents would quit throwing glances at him.

At last his dad could stand it no longer. He stood up and pulled Jerry to one side. "Jerry, aren't you entering anything *at all*?" he asked.

Jerry looked over at Garth's father. He thought he could see the man's ears sticking out, trying to hear them. "Yes," Jerry said, "the quarter mile."

"That the only one?"

Jerry wished his father would keep his voice low. "Yes, that's all," he said.

"Don't you think the others will call you a poor sport?" His dad was looking at him sternly now, and Jerry quivered. If only they would call the quarter mile!

"No, Dad," he said. "Just . . . gee, Dad, just trust me, won't you? Honest, I'll tell you all about it later."

His dad stared at him a moment, as if he wanted to see inside Jerry's brain. Jerry guessed that he was really hurting his father, but he looked back steadily.

"O.K., Jerry," his dad said at last. "I don't understand. Mother doesn't understand either. But of course we trust you. I guess you know what you're doing."

At last, as Jerry sat waiting by the fence, so nervous and excited that he almost felt sick, he heard: "First call for the final race—the quarter mile. This is a free-for-all.

The contestant will ride for a quarter of a mile, using any horse, any rig. Contestants will go to the starting line immediately."

Jerry jumped to his feet. "This is it, Dad," he gasped. "I'm in this one." He ran to Applesauce and pulled off the saddle. The old horse raised his head and looked at Jerry. "Applesauce!" Jerry whispered hurriedly. "This is what we've been waiting for. Shoot the works, boy. Let's show 'em." Applesauce nudged him gently, as though saying, "Relax, son. This is old stuff," and waited for him to mount.

But Jerry wanted to get his heavy boots off. He dropped to the ground and started pulling at them. Because of the heat the boots were tight. He pulled, he yanked, he tugged—and still they stuck.

"Last call for the quarter mile. Is everybody ready?" Mr. Williamson called.

"No, wait for me," Jerry yelled, struggling harder than ever. "Be there in a minute."

"What's the matter? What are you doing?" It was his dad. It was all right now, though. Even if Garth's father heard about it, it wouldn't matter.

"I'm riding bareback," Jerry gasped. "Help me with these boots. I'm riding like an Indian. Less weight the better."

Jerry's dad stared at him for a minute. Then he began to smile. His eyes lit up. He laughed aloud. "I see," he said. "Sure!" He turned around, grabbed Jerry's leg between his legs, and pulled the boot off. Then he grabbed the other boot, pulled hard, and Jerry jumped to his feet.

"Go it, boy," his dad said. "Forget anything I said. Ride like an Indian."

"I'll do my darnedest," Jerry smiled back, and vaulted easily across the pony's back. Applesauce's head came up, his ears jumped forward, and Jerry felt the familiar tensing of his muscles. He loped easily toward the others at the starting line.

"Well, I'll be. . . ." Ted looked at him. "Where did you learn that?"

"Sliding down haystacks," Jerry said.

All of them were watching him now, their faces full of amazement. He pulled the apaloosa in line with the others, but, to his surprise, Applesauce was jumpy. He was prancing, and when he finally got to the line he pawed the ground. All the dude horse in him had disappeared. He was a race horse—an Indian race horse—and he was ready to go.

"Hey, where's Garth?" Muriel asked, looking around.

"I'm coming."

They looked up and saw Garth riding up at a trot. He looked strange. Even his horse looked different. Then Jerry realized what had happened. Garth had stayed out of the last race, gone back to the saddle house, taken off all of Big Bay's trappings, and put on an English saddle.

Jerry's heart sank. He had hoped for so long that by riding bareback he would be lighter than the others and gain a few yards. But an English saddle weighed hardly anything. It was a real racing saddle, after all, and Garth was used to riding with it in the East. Jerry glanced at the others. Muriel was watching Garth as Big Bay pranced up to the starting line. Then she looked at Jerry and Applesauce. The others were doing the same thing. They had begun to realize that there were only two horses in the race—Big Bay, an Eastern type, a pure-bred American saddle horse, and Applesauce, the old, beat-up Indian pony.

Garth grinned at Jerry and said, "Good for you, Jerry. But I guessed it finally. I figured Sam must be teaching you something."

"He did his best," Jerry said, trying to smile. But he had lost some of his confidence. He looked down the field, saw the turn and the long pull back—twice around the oval for a complete race. It looked much longer, somehow, than the track Sam had staked out on the hayfield.

"Hey, Jerry!"

Jerry looked down and saw Sam standing below him with his grandfather. "Hi, Sam."

"All set?"

Jerry nodded, his lips tight.

"Look!" Sam held up something. "My grandfather says to give you this." Jerry saw a quirt made of heavy thong. "He says that on the last straightaway, wallop Applesauce with this across the rump."

"Won't it hurt him?" Jerry asked, alarmed. He had never done more than touch Applesauce with a switch.

"No. Grandfather says he's used to it. He expects it. He'll give you a little more speed at the very last."

Jerry hooked the loop of the quirt around his waist, so that he wouldn't lose it in the excitement of the race. Then he raised his eyes to the old Indian, who stood, tall and silent, next to his grandson. The old man looked at him without smiling, but Jerry saw the slight deepening of the wrinkles around his eyes and a very slight nod of the head, and this said all that needed saying—"You're riding for us. You're part of the dream."

"Now, I'm not going to shoot a pistol," Mr. Williamson was saying, "because it might scare some of these horses. I'll simply say, 'On your mark . . . get set . . . go. . . .' Now are you all ready?"

Jerry saw that while he had been dreaming, the others had been jockeying for position. Garth had the inside track, Ted was next, then Muriel. This put him close to the outside. He would have to cross over to the inside pretty fast or he would never get there at all.

"All right," said Mr. Williamson. *"On your mark!"*

From the corner of his eye, Jerry could see Garth hunched up on his English saddle, his feet short in the stirrups. Big Bay was sweating along his thick neck, and Jerry wondered if the horse was used to an English saddle and a jockey seat. Applesauce was quiet now, although Jerry could feel the muscles in his back like tight springs. Jerry lowered his hand on the reins slightly, and the apaloosa's ears flipped back, listening.

CHAPTER ELEVEN

Rides-like-an-Indian

In spite of his training, Jerry almost lost his seat. Applesauce seemed to take to the air. The hunched hind legs pushed and the front legs reached almost in one motion, and Applesauce rocketed ahead even faster than Jerry expected. For a second he hung on to the mane. Then he felt himself regain balance. He was loose, free, at home on the horse's back. He felt the smooth rhythm of the muscles, saw the mane flat against the pony's neck, the ears flat too, as Applesauce raced for the first turn. It was time to check his position.

Glancing behind him, Jerry saw that he was free. Those first few jumps had given him over 10 yards of start. The others were still crowded together, bunched up, fighting for position. Muriel's little mare was second, and she was trying to get on the inside, blocking Garth. Jerry moved Applesauce slowly toward the inside next to the "pole" as Sam called it. By the time he reached the turn, Applesauce was so close to the stakes marking it, that he was leaning into them, almost knocking them down. "Go it, boy," Jerry said. "Keep it up."

Now he was on the stretch leading to the crowd of dudes. He heard them yell as he went by. He saw his father, usually so dignified, jumping up and down like a madman, throwing his hat on the ground and jumping on it.

Jerry grinned into the wind and looked over his shoulder. They were strung out behind him now, and he saw Muriel, just entering the straightaway, losing ground fast. Some of the others were still bunched, and, as he watched, he saw Garth's big bay break out of them, gaining ground, gaining steadily.

Jerry turned away. He must save every inch of space on this corner. Every foot counted. Once again Applesauce leaned into the turn, moving within inches of the stakes without seeming to lose speed.

They flashed through the group where the finish line would be, but Jerry hardly noticed them, because, as they reached the next turn and Jerry looked over his shoulder, he saw that Garth was still gaining. He was free of all the others but Muriel, and he was passing her now, quite easily.

Again Applesauce hit the turn close to the stakes, but Jerry wondered whether the old horse was beginning to slow down just a little. He could feel the ribs pumping harder. The rhythm of the hoofbeats might be a tiny bit slower. Was Applesauce beginning to wear out? Was it too much for him after all?

It was then, just as they hit the next straightaway, that

Jerry heard the rattle of hoofs behind him. He turned long enough to see the big bay coming, gaining steadily, his great chest driving ahead, his heavy neck almost straight out. Garth was perched well forward, shouting encouragement into the horse's ears, and he was digging the horse with his spurs.

Applesauce must have heard Big Bay, too. Jerry felt the muscles stretch, the rhythm increase again. "Go it!" Jerry yelled into the wind. "Come on, Applesauce. Give, boy!" They had to reach the last turn before Garth. If he could gain a little or hold his own there, Jerry thought, there was only the final run to the finish.

He could hear Big Bay blowing now and could see the end of the horse's nose at his shoulder, as the horse continued to gain.

Then they hit the turn. The nose disappeared. Applesauce was doing the gaining now, saving every inch by hugging those stakes.

At last, through the dust, Jerry saw the finish ahead. It seemed a great distance away, with tiny figures watching, leaning over the edge of the track.

And the nose of Big Bay appeared again, then the thick neck and the black mane. He was coming up for sure this time, and there were no more corners. Jerry kicked Applesauce as hard as he could. He shouted at him. He begged. The two horses were almost neck and neck, and Jerry saw Garth, high on the horse's shoulders, his eyes slits against the dust.

As they entered the last 50 yards, Jerry felt Applesauce slow down slightly. He was still trying, Jerry thought . . . but . . . but. . . .

Then he remembered the quirt hanging limply from his wrist. He grabbed at it with his hand, missed, grabbed, caught it, and slammed it down across the apaloosa's flanks. Once, twice, he hit. He felt the flesh quiver, then a sudden increase in speed. The apaloosa's lungs seemed to burst. His nose seemed to reach out, every muscle stretched to the breaking point.

As the flag went down, Jerry knew that he had won by a nose, or by a part of a nose, maybe, but he had won. Then he felt Applesauce lurch, almost stagger.

Jerry didn't hear the cheers, the yells, or the applause. He didn't think of his father or Sam or the chief. All he knew was that he must get his weight off Applesauce as fast as possible. He dropped to the ground, hit running, fell, felt the rocks tear into his face, slid through the dust, and came to a stop in the middle of the track.

Although he could hear people running toward him, he paid no attention to them. What had happened to Applesauce? Had it been too much for him? Had he run his life away?

Jerry jumped to his feet and ran after his horse.

He found him at the turn, standing spraddle-legged, blowing foam from his mouth, his chest white with lather, his head down. Jerry pulled the split-ear bridle off and dropped the bit from the mouth to let the horse breathe

more freely. Then he threw his arms around the old apaloosa's neck. He was crying through the dust in his eyes, and he smelled the hot hide and rubbed his cheek against the sweaty neck. "Are you all right, Applesauce?" he begged. "Please be all right."

"Sure, he's all right," a deep voice said.

Jerry glanced up to see the crowd around him, and looking down on him was the tall Indian chief. "He's a good horse." The chief was smiling this time. No doubt about that. "Good Indian horse. Good Indian rider, too."

That night, as he and his father approached the campfire, Jerry heard the deep throbbing of tomtoms. The Indians had tightened the skins of their drums over the flames, and now they were beating on them, not loudly but steadily. Then came the low humming, a sort of wail, wavering into the night, as the drummers started to sing. Jerry looked up at the cold stars, sharp in the summer night. He saw the black rimrocks cutting into the sky, and he wondered how many years it had been since these mountains had heard the Indians sing.

Next he saw the wavering glow of the fire, making dancing shadows against the big cottonwoods and the three Indian tepees in the background. Then, as they joined the circle of dudes and guests from up and down the river, he saw, for the first time, the dancing Indians, nearly naked, wearing the war bonnets and headdresses of the tribe.

"It looks like the real thing," his dad said. "Does it make you feel like an Indian?"

"No." Jerry shook his head. "I guess I never could *feel* like one. I guess I just *dream* like one." He was not sure his father understood this. But it didn't matter. His dad had been pleased and happy about the race, delighted with the way he rode, and he had understood why he coul not break his promise to Sam, his blood brother.

As they worked their way into the circle of dudes, Jerry listened to the beat of the tomtoms grow faster, and he seemed to feel the throb of them in his bones. The wailing grew louder, and he saw the dancers increase their tempo. The old chief led, and behind him came several younger men, two squaws, and Sam with rings of bells around each ankle that jingled as he jumped and bent over, weaving and shouting, his body a shiny bronze in the firelight.

Jerry wished he were up there, too. He felt that he could do it, join it, enjoy it almost as much as the Indians did.

Then suddenly the tomtoms stopped. All the Indians except Sam sank back against the edges of their tepees, and the old chief, a well-known speaker for the Indians, stood in the firelight, staring over the silent crowd toward the distant peaks.

"It has been fine for us to come here," he said at last, in his deep voice. "It has been many moons since we were here before. Here in this valley in the old days, we hunted.

Here the buffalo came in the winter, because there was little snow and the food was good. We hunted the buffalo. You will find our tepee rings on the hills to prove it." He paused. "But that was long ago. Now the white man owns the land and we are friends with him. Yet today we saw something of which the Indians can be proud. A white man—a boy—raced an Indian horse trained on our reservation. We would like this boy to come to the fire."

Jerry, dreaming of dancing around the flames with bells on his ankles, failed to realize that the chief had called his name until he saw the others looking at him and he felt his father prod him. "Get out there, Jerry." He saw his dad's face smiling proudly in the firelight. "Get going. The chief wants you."

Jerry stood up. The chief pointed to his left, and Jerry walked over and stood next to Sam. He felt his legs quiver with a sudden weakness. He saw all the faces, lit by the fire, watching him, and for a moment he wanted to run away and hide in the woods. Then he looked at Sam standing proudly beside him, and he straightened. He knew that, even if he were frightened, he must look as tall and dignified as possible beside the Indian who was his brother.

"Today," said the chief, "this boy ran an Indian horse. He learned from my grandson to ride bareback as Indians ride . . . and we, the Indians, are proud of him. Not only because of this. But because he and my grandson have become blood brothers. They have performed the ceremony of keeping word. . . ."

Jerry saw the faces in front of him move. He heard the ripple of surprise as the ranch guests realized that he and Sam were blood brothers.

"For these two reasons we have decided in council to take this boy into our tribe," the chief went on, and Jerry saw Sam's smile widen into a happy grin.

"But first," the chief said, "I ask that a song be sung, telling of this race and of how the white boy rode for the Indians." As he spoke, a young Indian stood up and walked close to the campfire and began to sing a low wailing kind of song that rose and fell until it echoed from the rimrock. At first, Jerry had a hard time realizing that this was a song about him. But as the song rose in intensity, he felt his heart start to beat rapidly, and he knew that, although the words were strange, they had the feeling of the race in them, the feeling of excitement he had felt that afternoon.

Finally, the young Indian stopped and faded back into the shadows.

"Now," said the chief, stepping up to Jerry, "I hereby proclaim you a member of the tribe." He held out something, and Jerry, half dazed with the excitement, took it. He saw that it was a beaded headband with a feather in it, and, with Sam's help, he put it on, feeling it tight against his forehead. Then, at last, he began to realize what had happened. The dream—what had seemed an impossible dream—had come true. He was as near being an Indian as any white man could be, nearer than Garth, nearer even than Chuck, the great bronc rider.

"In our tribe, you now have the name of Rides-like-an-Indian," the chief intoned. "You are to stand in a place of honor at my right." He pointed majestically, and Jerry walked over and stood to the right of the chief. "When you are grown," he added, looking down at Jerry, "you will have an honored place among the council of elders and smoke the pipe of peace with them."

At last the chief signaled that the ceremony was over. All the dudes applauded, and Jerry found himself shaking hands with the chief and with Sam. Then the drums started, and the Indians began to dance again.

Soon the dudes joined, and Jerry found himself following Sam, trying to do the steps he was doing. Now and then Sam would turn, singing the Indian wail, the bells on his ankles jingling, and grin at him, saying, Jerry thought, "How is it with you my brother, Rides-like-an-Indian?"

It was a long and exciting night, and after the campfire had burned down into embers and the dudes had left, Jerry was still wide-awake. He walked back to the ranch and, instead of going to his cabin, drifted down to the wranglers' corral, where Applesauce was enjoying his reward by stuffing himself with hay. The horse heard the footsteps, and as Jerry climbed the fence and hooked his heels in the middle rail, the apaloosa's welcoming whinny echoed toward the stars. Applesauce left the hay pile and ambled over, ruffling his nose and asking for more oats.

"No more," Jerry said, leaning over and scrubbing the

old horse between the ears. "Chuck says that more than a quart would not be good for you."

Jerry sat there dreaming to his heart's content and failed to hear Sam until the Indian appeared beside him on the fence. "I heard Applesauce nicker," Sam said. "I thought you must be down here, my brother."

"Gee, what a day," Jerry said. "This was the best day of my whole life."

"It was a good one for me, too," Sam said. "I picked up a new job."

"A new job?" Jerry asked. "What is it?"

"I'm a dude wrangler now," Sam said, laughing softly. "And a horse wrangler, too. The boss took me aside and told me that from now on, someone else can do the chores."

"Gee, that's swell," Jerry said. Now they could see more of each other, he thought. Now they'd both be part of the gang.

"And most of the time I'm to teach kids to ride bareback," Sam went on, chuckling softly. "And do you know who my first pupil is going to be?"

"Who?"

"It's hard to believe," Sam said, slapping his leg, "but darned if my very first student isn't Garth!"